66670000020206

A LOVE DENIED

1815: Felix, Earl of Chando, sets out to engage a suitable companion for his much-loved mother. He finds her in Miss Phoebe Allen, whose charm and good nature win him over. Once at Elwood, Phoebe also takes on the muddled household accounts, and advises Felix on how he can save the ailing estate. Felix finds himself falling in love with her — but he is determined never to marry, as he fears there is bad blood in his family. Will Phoebe change his mind?

Books by Louise Armstrong
in the Linford Romance Library:

HOLD ON TO PARADISE
JAPANESE MAGIC
A PICTURE OF HAPPINESS
THE PRICE OF HAPPINESS
CONCRETE PROPOSAL
PATTERN OF LOVE
KINGFISHER DAYS
MASTER OF DIPLOMACY
HER GUARDIAN ANGEL
LOVE'S GAMBLE
ALTERED IMAGES

LOUISE ARMSTRONG

A LOVE DENIED

Complete and Unabridged

LINFORD
Leicester

First published in Great Britain in 2015

First Linford Edition
published 2017

*A catalogue record for this book is available
from the British Library.*

ISBN 978-1-4448-3146-7

Published by
F. A. Thorpe (Publishing)
Anstey, Leicestershire

Set by Words & Graphics Ltd.
Anstey, Leicestershire
Printed and bound in Great Britain by
T. J. International Ltd., Padstow, Cornwall

This book is printed on acid-free paper

1

Soft silver rain had been falling all day, but now the clouds had cleared to reveal a gorgeous late summer evening. Outside, the birds sang joyously of sunshine and freedom; inside the air was stifling. Felix George Edmund Henry, seventh Earl of Chando, looked at his mother's pink face.

'You look hot, dearest,' he said, smiling affectionately at her.

His mother grimaced at the apple-wood logs that blazed in the stone fireplace.

'I would like some air,' she agreed.

Felix rose from the carved chair where he had been sitting at the side of his mother's bed. He had to skirt a screen that had been embroidered by Mary Queen of Scots before he could reach the ground-floor window. Red velvet curtains, padded against the winter cold and wonderfully swagged and festooned, almost obscured the stone embrasure. Felix fought his way through the lavish and rather dusty crimson drapes and flung open the leaded-glass window.

Sunlight and sweet clean air flowed into the room. He leaned his forehead on the stone of the window embrasure and looked out. The rolling parkland that swelled up and away towards the Lancashire coastline looked fresh and green. Tiny in the distance, a team of horses ploughed a field, sea gulls swooping around them. The patchwork of fields looked tidily prosperous. His list of essential tasks never seemed to get shorter, but at least, as the view from this window proved, he was restoring order to the estate at last.

'What an enormous sigh, darling,' commented the sweet voice of his mother.

He swung around and smiled at her. 'I'm sorry, Mama. That was very rude of me, but it is quarter day tomorrow.'

Georgiana, Dowager Countess of Chando, had emerald-green eyes exactly the same shape and colour as her son's. Their green depths were full of love and sympathy as she gazed at him.

'You spend too much time on the estate, my love.'

'I do no more than what should be done, indeed, what urgently must be done.'

His mother gave him a glance of perfect understanding, and then looked away, for they were coming perilously close to the awkward subject of just who had left the estate in tatters and exactly why the latest earl was having to work so hard at putting it back in order. Georgiana changed the topic.

'My dear, when would you be thinking of renovating the Dower House?'

Felix laughed.

'Is that a subtle hint? I shall not be ousting you in favour of a new bride any time soon.'

Georgiana's dark brows winged down as she worried.

'Have you no thoughts of marriage at all?'

Felix had no intention of telling his mother that he was violently opposed to the idea of marriage. Instead he would give her a valid reason for staying single.

'The estate is in no position to support a bride.'

'My dear, if it were a case of true love — '

'I cast aside all such romantic notions when I left the army.'

His mother bit her lip.

'It's a shame that you had to leave, but the estate was in such a desperate position . . . '

Again she choked off her words, and a charged silence fell.

Only loyalty and a consciousness of what was due to her husband, the late earl, prevented Georgiana from saying aloud what she and her son both knew to be true: it had been a blessing and a relief when the earl had broken his neck while he was out fox hunting.

The estate had been on the brink of disaster. One more losing session at cards would have seen them all in the poorhouse. But now Felix was home, and the new earl was slowly restoring the fields and the woods, the farms and the moors, and the rivers and the mines into the thriving and prosperous concerns they should be.

Felix wished he could call his complaint back. It was true that a thick fog seemed to have cut him off from life, fun and enjoyment since he had exchanged the freedom and excitement of campaigning in Spain, in favour of rents, mortgages and an endless daily grind, but he didn't want to admit how dull he found his life.

'How was Aunt Eugenie?' he asked hastily. 'It was very good of you to journey all that way to see your sister, although I must say, the change seems to have done you good.'

His mother's green eyes dimmed sadly.

'She is very poorly, I'm afraid.'

'Ah,' Felix said, realising that he'd chosen the wrong subject if he was hoping to cheer up his mother.

Georgiana nodded.

'Because she is so ill, I could not refuse her request, which means, my darling boy, another task for you.'

She gestured to an embroidered hanging that was lying on an inlaid table next to her bed. Tiny colourful stitches detailed the Chando family tree.

'The family details are not complete. While she was putting her affairs in order, Eugenie found out that her husband's sister, Arabella, did not die a spinster without issue, as we all believed.'

'No?'

His mother's eyes sparkled and she leaned towards her son.

'Listen to the story Eugenie told me: the true fact of the matter is that Arabella ran off with a curate, married him, and had a little girl before she died.'

'You have unearthed a family secret!'

'Eugenie showed me two letters from Arabella, one giving the details of the marriage and begging for forgiveness, and the other announcing the birth of the child. They were such pretty letters. How hard-hearted the family must have been to ignore them.'

The door clicked, and a footman bowed in Miss Thalia Belmont, who trotted into the room in her usual scurry.

'Oh, Chando! What a surprise to see you visiting your mama. It must be at least a week since you came to see us. She never complains, but the hours pass so slowly when one is confined to a chair. It's a pity you are not able to spend more time with your mother. You seem to find so many, many excuses to spend your time about the estate. I declare we hardly ever see you.'

Felix kept his face composed, but he couldn't hide his eyes. Georgiana cast a quick look at his expression, and then turned to her companion.

'Cousin Thalia, dear. I have a fancy for a baked egg for dinner and I know Chef has something far grander in train. I depend on your tact. Could you possibly . . . '

The gooseberry eyes goggled, the companion drew another breath and she bleated: 'Well, of course I will, cousin. I am perfectly able to do any little errand. It is a pity that you did not inform me before, because I have just walked past the kitchen, and I have the tiniest blister upon the heel of my foot, but I am quite able to walk all the way back to the kitchen, if you insist.'

Felix marvelled at his mother's charm as she smiled and said gently, 'Thank you so much, Thalia.'

Miss Belmont trotted back to the door, upsetting a gilt chair as she went. The footman held the door open and she scurried out.

'Thank you for sending her away, Mama. I don't know which is worse: what she says or the bleating voice she says it in.'

The dowager countess sighed.

'She's very well meaning.'

Felix thought she was poison, and one barb had gone home.

'Mama, do you get lonely?'

'I do.'

Despite having asked the question, Felix was utterly dumbfounded by her answer. Never in his life had he heard his mama admit to the slightest unhappiness; she never complained about anything. Had he heard her correctly?

Her green eyes were smiling a little, perhaps at his stunned expression.

'I have been feeling increasingly lonely, especially during the long dark winters,' she admitted frankly, 'and that is why I need you to carry out Eugenie's request.'

'I'll do whatever I can.'

'The notion that Arabella's daughter may be in difficult circumstances is preying on my sister's mind. Eugenie has such a tender heart, poor thing, and all the original parties to the quarrel are dead, so there can be no objections to her righting this ancient wrong. She has arranged for a settlement and she wants the girl found so that it may be bestowed on her.'

'That's not a problem, Mama. The lawyer shall find her for you.'

His mother turned her lovely green eyes to him in appeal.

'I had thought that you . . . '

'What can I do that the lawyer can't?'

'I own I yearn for company. It's been growing in my mind that Eugenie's niece might come to live with me.'

'There's no saying what kind of a person she may turn out to be.'

His mother raised a white hand and waved aside his warning.

'She may be a clod or a bore or a prig and a bluestocking,' Felix insisted. 'Beware of creating a fantasy figure, Mother.'

'I suppose you're right,' Georgiana said.

Unable to bear the disappointment in her green eyes, Felix touched her shoulder gently.

'But she may be the company you need,' he said, smiling. 'If it pleases you, Mama, the girl shall be found and we shall see if she will make a congenial companion for you.'

* * *

Footman Peter Fletcher's favourite job in the whole world was to mind the scoreboard while his master played billiards. That afternoon, he was lounging by the window, languidly keeping track of the shots, enjoying the delicious August weather. Despite the blazing sun outside, it was cool in the long room.

A soft click of ivory as the last ball flew into the pockets was followed by a laugh.

'Dash it, Chando. Let's play again! I'll beat you in the next game.'

Peter looked at the master's friend, Robin Hathaway, and reflected that you never saw two men more opposite:

Robin was as jolly and fair as Felix was dark and grim. The footman liked Robin. Some said he was tactless, but you knew where you were with him and he was open-handed when it came to tipping.

'That's the last game.'

'You can't refuse me another match,' Robin protested.

'I'm afraid I'll have to. I must leave to carry out an assignment.'

Robin's blue eyes flew open in surprise.

'Not a woman?'

Felix laughed.

'Probably not in the way you are thinking, but yes, a woman.'

'Don't be so irritating,' Robin advised crisply. 'Tell me the tale.'

Peter was enthralled as Felix recounted the story of the Cinderella niece. It was all news to him, and to the other servants, he'd be bound. He couldn't wait to enlighten them!

'You must be touched in the top storey,' Robin said to his friend, shaking his head with a laugh. 'This mystery niece is bound to be most peculiar. Still, it's a change for you to be going out hunting for a woman. You spend most of your time running away from women determined to marry you.'

'They would soon change their tune if they knew how shabby the estate was.'

Robin gave Felix a sympathetic buffet on his shoulder.

'It's improving, thanks to your hard work. You deserve a rest. Why don't we take a break in town? You can send your lawyer chappie to look for the girl.'

'Caldicott has already found her. The curate, a Mr Allen, returned to his home town in Essex, where he married the runaway Arabella. She presented him with the daughter in question and then she died. The curate lived long enough to bring up the girl, it seems, but then he died, leaving this Miss Phoebe Allen penniless.'

'My stars! What kind of a name is Phoebe?'

'If you had chanced to open a book when we were up at Oxford, you would know that it was a classical name.'

'She'll be a bluestocking,' prophesised Robin. 'How could she be otherwise? Leave it to Caldicott to play fairy godfather, and we'll go to London.'

'If it was just the settlement, I would, but Mama has got a maggot in her head: she thinks Arabella's daughter would make her a companion. I think as you do, how can the girl be anything but frightful, given her background? But it's not a judgement I can ask Caldicott to make. I'll have to go myself. I do not wish Mama to find herself burdened with another Thalia Belmont.'

'Why is it that female companions are always blisters?'

'Phoebe Allen is not a companion.'

'You astonish me! I thought poor relations were always companions.'

'Not this one. It seems she has some kind of employment at a school.'

Robin shuddered.

'She's a schoolmarm? That's even worse.'

'It does not look promising,' agreed Felix. 'Caldicott says she has a position at a seminary for young ladies.'

'Young ladies, eh?' Robin sat bolt upright and tidied his blond curls. 'I'd better come with you, as a chaperone, don't you know?'

Felix shook his head firmly. Robin examined him closely.

'I haven't seen that kind of wicked glint in your eyes since we were at Salamanca. Stars, what larks we had! Do you remember the night we stole the captain's shaving kit? But I digress. What are you thinking?'

'I need to inspect this girl, discreetly, and see what kind of a person she is before she is asked to visit Elwood.'

Yes, the footman reflected to himself in the silence that followed, no matter how ghastly they were, you couldn't turn out your relatives once they had their feet under the table. As usual, his master had the right of it.

'What are you going to do?' probed Robin.

Felix looked oddly defensive as he replied, 'I got to thinking of our scouting missions . . . '

Robin laughed out loud.

'My word, you always did like a masquerade. Come on, what disguise are you planning for this little adventure?'

'I thought I would enquire if the school were looking for a classics master. It would give me the opportunity to determine Phoebe Allen's nature.'

'When do we start?'

'You're not coming!'

Glee lit Robin's blue eyes until they sparkled like sapphires.

'Oh yes I am. You are not leaving me out of a junket like this. Of course I'm coming with you. Hie, Peter, are you still here? Well, you can make yourself useful. Where can we get some dressing-up clothes?'

2

In April of 1812, Miss Ada Penny-feather took a lease on a school building in the town of Dagenham, and was nearly ruined when no young ladies joined her seminary. Luckily, the good aldermen of the city were looking for an establishment suitable for the care of abandoned female children and an agreement was soon reached.

The school was so centrally located that the tradesmen delivered. When the maid, Betsy Jones, heard a hammering on the oak door of the school at three o'clock one wet afternoon, she hoped it would be the muffin man.

She opened the door and a gust of wind blew into the hall. The same wind caught the coat of the magnificent male personage who stood there, blowing the dark folds of his cape. He looked so tall that he seemed to fill the doorway. He took a step forward, shook silver drops of rain out of his dark hair, and gazed at her with emerald eyes.

'Is your mistress home? I wish to enquire about employment.'

At the sound of his deep resonant voice Betsy's wits deserted her; her legs quivered and, as she told her best friend Maisie later, her knees just folded all by themselves and she dropped into a curtsey that was more like a tumble onto the stone flags of the hall. Ostrich-like, she threw her white apron over her head and hoped that someone would come to rescue her.

Robin Hathaway was chuckling as he moved forward, but he did lower his voice before muttering in his friend's ear.

'I told you your disguise was rotten, Chando. I don't think that's the kind of greeting a would-be schoolmaster usually gets.'

'Hush!'

Felix's green eyes flashed as he quelled Robin with a glare, making him look, had he but known it, more rather than less imperious.

Little Susie Carter, who acted as the tweeny maid, came out to see what had happened to the muffins. She, too, took one stunned look at the personage standing in the doorway, and sank onto her knees on the ground next to Betsy.

'It's not going to work, Chando,' Robin advised, looking at the two overcome maids. 'I told you that it would take more than lawyer Caldicott's old clothes to make you look like a schoolmaster. Better change your story.'

A rush and patter of footsteps heralded the appearance of two dozen or more rosy-cheeked girls in matching grey skirts and white pinafores. At the sight of two gentlemen of quality in the doorway, they fell to the floor in sweet curtseys. They soon bobbed up again, smiling; but then they saw that Susie and Betsy were still curtseying low, so, with a rustle of skirts the girls quickly bobbed down again. Ripples of laughter showed how much fun they were having.

Robin glanced at the expression on Felix's face and laughed out loud.

'Surely you're not afraid of a few schoolgirls? Why, man, I've seen you take on a pack of French bandits single-handed.'

'Brigands don't giggle!' Felix snapped.

'What a lark!' replied Robin, wiping away tears of laughter. 'Oh, here we go: this must be Miss Pennyfeather.'

Both men turned to watch a lady in rather wonderful old-fashioned black bombazine sweep into the hall. She was indeed the proprietor, but she took one look at Felix, emitted a distinct squawk, and fell to the floor in a tangle of crinoline and hoops.

'This has got to stop!' declared Felix, surveying the female sea of giggling, bowing, curtseying, bobbing and prone figures on the stone floor.

'Girls!' said a low, clear voice.

The giggles died instantly. The little girls became as still and silent as a flock of sleeping doves.

Felix stared at the small personage who had just entered the hall. She was dressed exactly as the girls were, in a dove-grey dress covered by a white pinafore. Her dark hair was pulled back into a workaday arrangement. She was dressed like a Quaker, or a servant, nothing, nothing like a lady at all. Yet the very plainness of her outfit meant that it faded into the background and he was conscious only of her heart-shaped face, rosebud mouth and grey eyes as calm as water. Personality radiated from the tips of her neat little feet to the top of her self-possessed head.

She swept him a beautiful curtsey, and returned to her full height in a graceful swoop, saying as she did so, 'my lord.'

Then she turned to the prone figures.

'Katie and Nellie, get up! Now, take yourself over to Miss Pennyfeather, one of you under each elbow and ups-a-daisy. Now, girls, snip snap. It's rude to stand about staring. Go into the drawing room for Bible studies.'

The hall fluttered with skirts and aprons as the little girls got to their feet and scrambled off. The owner of the tart voice nodded after them approvingly, and then turned to Miss Pennyfeather. That lady was attempting to shake down her acres of black skirt over the hoops of her old-fashioned crinoline. She was goggling at Felix as if he were a wild lion who was going to pounce on her and gobble her up.

'Take the gentlemen to your parlour, Miss Pennyfeather,' Phoebe advised her employer kindly. 'I will send in Betsy with the tea tray.'

A piercing scream from the back region of the house cut her off.

'There's a spider in my mixing bowl!' hollered a female voice. 'Miss Phoebe! Save me!'

Phoebe's bright eyes flashed with merriment.

'Cook will give notice if I don't rescue her. Do pray excuse me.'

And with a swirl of grey skirt, she was gone.

Miss Pennyfeather cast one startled look at Felix and scuttled out of the hall.

Felix stared around the suddenly-empty hall and then looked back at his friend.

'Robin, we are leaving!'

'What about Miss Allen? Don't you want to get acquainted and find out if your mother would like her?'

'A person from this madhouse couldn't possibly suit . . . what are you laughing at?'

Robin was helpless with giggles.

'I do not suppose that you were ever spurned in favour of a spider before.'

'This is a most unconventional household,' Felix replied, a little stiffly.

Felix turned to the door, but someone was holding down the cape of his coat. He whipped around, looked down, and was stunned to see a small girl. She regarded him with hope in her brown eyes.

'Are you a fairy godfather?' she trilled.

She was dressed in plain grey as all the girls were but pretty golden ringlets tumbled over her shoulders and her bright dark eyes sparkled over rose-petal cheeks.

'I am not,' he said, but his voice was gentle.

Robin looked at the little girl, smiling.

'Oh, yes he is a fairy godfather.'

The little girl looked thrilled and clutched Felix's coattails even tighter. Felix glared at Robin.

'What did you say that for?'

A smile lit Robin's blue eyes.

'So far as Miss Allen is concerned, the role of fairy godfather is exactly yours,' he pointed out.

Felix scowled at his friend, and was about to ask him if he'd taken leave of his senses, but the little girl tugged firmly on his coat.

'We all want to go to the fair!' she announced.

Giving in, Felix knelt on the stone flags so that she could speak to him more easily.

'Why should you not?'

Dimples formed in each rosy cheek as she smiled.

'Because it costs one farthing each to go into Farmer Rose's field where the fair is being held and there are sixty-eight of us. We need one shilling and five pence.'

Felix was stunned.

'One shilling and five pence?' he repeated incredulously.

'It's right,' she told him earnestly. 'Miss Phoebe said my sums were right.'

'It's not your calculations,' Felix replied and then stopped, realising that it was impossible to explain that he was stunned to hear that the dearest wish of sixty-eight people could be satisfied by the trifling sum of one shilling and five pence.

Robin began counting on his own fingers and then gave up.

'You must be jolly good at sums,' he

said admiringly.

'Miss Phoebe teaches us sums. She teaches Bible studies as well, and she says we may not ask God for little things like going to the fair. But I think fairy godfathers must be different. It is all right to ask you, isn't it, sir?'

Displaying the forethought and presence of mind that had made him such a good companion to go on a war campaign with, Robin tapped his friend on the shoulder and slid a large golden half-guinea into his hand.

Felix smiled.

'Your fairy godfather will grant your wish. Close your eyes and hold out your hands.'

The little mite screwed up her eyes tight and took a deep breath. Felix gently placed the coin in her hand.

'You may look now.'

The little girl opened her eyes and gazed down at the golden coin. A brilliant smile illuminated her face.

The rustle of a dove-grey skirt heralded the return of Miss Phoebe

Allen. She took in the golden coin and the obvious delight on the little girl's face, and then she looked at the two men with a wide, frank smile.

'That was kind of you. The whole school has been longing to go to the fair. They are good children, on the whole, but there is little money for treats. Say thank you to the kind gentlemen, Clover.'

Clover lifted a face still radiant with the magic of fairy gold.

'Thank you, Fairy Godfather. Please, can I go and tell the others?'

'You may,' Felix said, smiling as he returned to his full height.

'I'm so sorry that you have been left to wait,' Phoebe said, sweeping another exquisite curtsey. 'I'm sorry I had to leave you but I couldn't allow Cook to be upset or we'd all go hungry. I can cook a little, but dinner for so many people is beyond me.'

'Sixty-eight people I believe,' Robin said with a smile in his voice.

She nodded.

'Exactly so, but do please follow me.'

Felix held up a hand to stop her.

'We don't need to trouble Miss Pennyfeather. I have found out all that I need to know.'

One dark eyebrow winged up in surprise. Felix had had time to revise his cover story and it seemed a pity to waste it, so he smiled at her and said, 'The fact is that I was misinformed as to the nature of your school. It is not a foundling that I wished to place, but the daughter of an acquaintance who particularly desired that his daughter be taught no mathematics.'

Phoebe nodded.

'There is nothing worse than forcing a child to study.'

'If you understand that, then you are a teacher above pearls and rubies,' Robin agreed, fervently.

She gave him a sympathetic look.

'Did you have a tough time at school?'

'I still bear the scars.'

She smiled.

'On behalf of my orphans I do thank you. They will remember meeting their fairy godfather for many years.'

Felix couldn't resist lingering a moment to examine the unusual woman who stood in front of him.

'And you will go to the fair with them?' he asked.

'I most certainly shall,' she agreed, and the smile that lit up her face was as radiant as little Clover's.

Despite her undoubted air of authority, she looked like a happy six-year-old. Felix gazed at her, astonished that the simple prospect of a trip to the fair could make her so happy. He was feeling a strange reluctance to leave. He realised that he hadn't yet broken the news of her changed fortune to this most unusual girl. He looked down at her smooth face and wide forehead. She smiled back at him with calm goodwill in her grey eyes.

'What time will you go to the fair?' he demanded.

'Not until after prayers.'

'I expect we shall meet with you, and your charges, again later, as we shall be attending the fair.'

'We shall?' Robin gasped, too astonished to be tactful, and then he caught himself. 'Oh, yes, quite. I always enjoy a good fair myself.'

Felix found that he could leave, now that he knew when and where he would be seeing Miss Phoebe Allen again.

'My compliments to Miss Pennyfeather and my apologies for disturbing her,' he said, stepping into the high street.

Felix felt happy for the first time since that black November day four years ago when he had walked into his father's study and picked up the first of the thousands of bills that needed paying. He noticed that the air was fine and fresh and the sun shone from behind gleaming white clouds. A flock of geese waddled squawking down the centre of the road, the goose girl in hot pursuit. A farmer led a plough horse towards the forge that stood on the corner of the street. As they walked by, they could see a small boy using bellows to blow up the glowing red fire.

Robin's shoulders were shaking.

'Miss Pennyfeather's face!' he gasped. 'And a spider!'

The two men had to conduct themselves with decorum while they were walking up the main street in public view, so they managed to maintain straight faces as they turned in through the stone arch of the coaching yard and through the reception area of the Lamb, but once safely in the private parlour that joined their two bedrooms, they fell upon the landlady's much-prized upholstered chairs and roared with laughter as they relived the event.

In fact they laughed so long and so loudly that the innkeeper sent up the boots to see if the either of the gentlemen was having a funny turn, and if they needed any brandy.

3

After the two visitors left, Phoebe found herself holding her stomach and staring at the wood panels of the closed oak door. She was trying to work out how she felt.

A loud puffing and panting and the sparking of stout boots on the stone floor announced the arrival of William Ploughman.

'I'm that riled with myself for not being here to open the door.'

'You were busy catching rabbits, William, and that was a task of far greater importance, because it's the end of the month and there's nothing else to eat!'

William's dark eyes sparkled with pleasure.

'Aye, well, I caught us some nice fat bunnies. But it's downright aggravating! The hours I spend on duty and when have we ever had gentlemen visitors before?'

'Never,' said Phoebe, feeling sad and shaking her head.

'Can't be helped, I suppose. Well, I need to see about coal for schoolroom fire.'

William stumped off about his duties, but Phoebe didn't follow his example. The exchange with a gentleman, brief as it had been, had stirred emotions that were deep and private, that had to do with the life that she'd lost.

She never allowed herself to think of life with her papa. It was territory that had been untouched for years. It frightened her that a total stranger — belatedly she realised that she'd no idea what the names of the visitors were — should elicit such powerful feelings.

The gentleman, whoever he had been, had examined her face so critically, so closely. His green eyes had never seemed to leave her face. She wasn't used to such attention. She was just Phoebe, carer and worker and solver of problems. Nobody saw her as a person anymore, but this man had. He'd seemed to be looking deeper than her features, and she felt as if he'd seen deep into her soul and unearthed her deepest secret: that sometimes she yearned to be free and regretted the life that was lost to her.

A wail rose from the schoolroom.

'Miss Phoebe, Sally's been sick.'

'Coming, lovely,' Phoebe called, rushing off for a bucket of water.

As she bustled around her myriad duties, the image of the children's fairy godfather kept flashing into her mind. She'd had to look up to see his face; he stood at least six foot high. His broad shoulders and lean hips suggested a man who led an active life; she guessed that he would ride, and shoot and probably box and fence as well. Who was he? What did he do? Despite the look of a soldier which hung about him, his skin wasn't tanned, just healthily glowing, which suggested he was not currently in the army or navy. Yet there was that small scar on his cheek that gave him such a mysterious air. Surely he'd had adventures?

And his eyes! She'd never seen any like them. They were green, a lovely glowing green, as green as sunshine through glass. And they had probed with a grave intensity that was frightening, and yet they had laughed and shared fun in the next blink. It had been hard to look away from him, and even harder to control the wild beating of her heart.

Phoebe's thoughts shied away from the troubling subject of how the man made her feel, to the more concrete mystery of his presence on her doorstep. The teacher in her scented the phoniness of his story. What possible chain of events could lead to a young gentleman, for gentleman he clearly was, to look for a school for someone else's relative? She scented some kind of lark or a fraud. Then she rejected the idea of a fraud. The golden half-guinea he'd left behind was proof of his good intentions, and everything in his bearing proclaimed him to be a proud and upright man.

It must have been some kind of lark, then. He was involved in a joke or a prank of some kind. She knew that young men with plenty of money and nothing to do were prone to mischief, yet he had such a serious face. Oh well, it was no business of hers. She just hoped that he had not realised how nervous and uncertain he had made her feel. It seemed important that he not know how dramatic his impact on her had been, and even more important that she should not feel so unsettled by the man again. If he should turn up at the fair, she would keep tight control of her feelings.

Her heart skipped with excitement at the idea of a jaunt, but it was time for mathematics, and the fair must be forgotten for the moment. Phoebe managed to concentrate, but it was too much to ask of the little girls.

'Aren't you looking forward to the

fair, Miss Phoebe?'

'I am!' she admitted frankly. 'But I want you all to stop tumbling about like a basket of kittens and settle to your sums.'

'We can't think about sums!' they wailed.

'Oh? Then how will we know how much gingerbread each person can buy with the change from the fairy gold?'

Silence fell. Her young charges bent their heads over their slates. Phoebe watched them as they muttered, figured and counted, but instead of working on the household accounts, she thought of the mysterious caller until dinner time.

Cook must have recovered from her shock with the spider because she made a delicious rabbit pie and she conjured up a rice pudding to follow, so everyone was feeling content and well-fed as they lined up in the hall after the meal.

Phoebe had little time for beautification, but she tied up her bonnet with brand-new pansy-purple ribbons. When a little voice inside her whispered that maybe wanting to look pretty for the fairy godfather wasn't a good idea, she tuned it out. Didn't she always try to look nice? But in her heart, she knew that the previous encounter had made her feel more feminine, more inclined to wear ribbons, and that was a strangely sweet feeling.

'We're ready, Miss Phoebe!' called the girls.

Phoebe asked Kitty to walk next to her. Kitty was fully trained and ready to take up a position as a lady's maid. The older girl could be trusted to keep her wits and to help if any kind of mayhem broke out, as it surely would in all the excitement of a fair.

William, beaming in his best green waistcoat, opened the creaking door onto a beautiful summer evening. Miss Pennyfeather, smelling strongly of juniper berries but quite steady on her feet, led the way, and the girls filed after her. Next came the maids in all their finery, then Cook in a splendid black hat decorated with cherries. Sixty-eight persons all present and correct.

The road was busier than usual because so many people were heading for the fair. Phoebe's insides were trembling. She was determined not to look for him. She walked demurely past the forge, keeping her eyes down, registering the glow of the fire out of the corner of her eye. The next business was Mr Clegg's seed shop. She glanced at the glass of the bow-fronted window, and, with an impact like a blow, she saw the reflected image of a tall dark figure and a shorter blond one waiting on the other side of the road. There was no mistake. It couldn't be anyone but the fairy godfather. He looked so different from the ordinary citizens hurrying to the fair.

He puzzled her. He was a mass of contradictions. His hair was a rich, thick shock of mahogany brown. Phoebe might be immured in an orphanage, but she was feminine enough to know that his artfully tousled locks had been textured by a stylist rather than the wind, and that his haircut was a lot more fashionable than his clothes. So which was the real man? She looked again. He'd seen her and was crossing the street.

In that split second Phoebe realised that he made her feel insecure. Anxiety was an unpleasant feeling connected with the dark days after her father died. Insecurity had no part of her life at Miss Pennyfeather's. This was her world and in it, she knew that she reigned like a queen. She drew herself up to her full five feet two inches and kept her gaze away from him, but the nerve-endings of her skin told her that he was bowing politely to Miss Pennyfeather and walking past the orphanage crocodile towards her.

She watched his progress under her lashes. His sangfroid did not desert him under the pressure of returning the little girls' greetings, but there was a distinct blush and an uneasy grin on the face of his blond companion.

When he reached her, the handsome

man stopped, turned, and fell into step beside her. It was as if he had been waiting for her, and only her, all along. She cast a glance at his face and met vivid green eyes looking back. It was hard to breathe suddenly. The slow sweep of his inspection made her want to squirm. There was a masculine force in him that made her feel vulnerable. Reacting against it, she turned to his companion, who had the kind of merry face you'd like in a brother, and was completely unalarming.

'We do not know the names of our kind benefactors,' she said.

Her mouth was dry and she heard her words echoing oddly in her ears, which made her feel awkward and stupid.

The blond man bowed.

'Robin Hathaway, at your service, and this is my friend, Felix Chando.'

Phoebe smiled at Robin, very aware of the dark man, Mr Chando, watching her face. She caught his green gaze and then wished she hadn't. The muscles of her face would no longer support a smile and she suffered an inner jolt that made her heart catch.

She was glad to hear excited screams from the girls. It gave her the opportunity to turn away from him. A gipsy was stamping towards them beating a drum, calling to people to visit the fair. Tied to the man by a long chain was a monkey in a red jacket. The beast was prancing at the end of its chain, chattering and gibbering at the orphans. Half of the girls were calling to the monkey to come to them, the other half were shrinking away in fear.

'Back in line, please,' she called.

The girls obeyed immediately.

When she looked back at the mysterious Mr Chando, his expression held surprise, pleasure and masculine judgement.

'You have them well drilled,' he remarked approvingly.

Phoebe lifted her chin and tried to steady herself.

'They are good girls,' she replied, the

words feeling like cotton wool in her mouth.

In truth they were all in some danger of tripping over their clogs as they kept turning back to sneak little glances at the marvellous fairy godfather who was walking with Miss Phoebe.

Robin smiled and waved a hand at the curious girls.

'My stars, I'd rather be stared at by the French cavalry.'

'Oh? Were you in the war?' Phoebe cried. 'Did you know the Duke of Wellington?'

Robin smiled.

'Chando here was Wellesley's right-hand man.'

Phoebe was thrilled to her toes.

'The Duke of Wellington is my greatest hero. There is a kind of style in all that he does that is most attractive!'

'Well said!' Robin cried.

But Felix gave her a half smile. She wished he hadn't. She couldn't look away from the curve of his mouth.

'You are not at all what I expected,'

he said thoughtfully, almost challengingly. 'The Duke is an odd choice of hero for a schoolmarm.'

'And how many schoolmarms do you know?' Phoebe flashed.

That lazy half-smile curved again.

'You cannot be typical.'

'If that was meant as a compliment, then you missed, sir. A schoolmarm must be well acquainted with politics and current affairs.'

Silence fell. Phoebe wondered if she'd shocked him with her blunt reply. Perhaps she shouldn't have fired up so, but something about the man provoked the very depths of her heart. In order to escape thoughts of him, she looked ahead to check on her charges. The crocodile was now proceeding down a muddy road that had sweet-scented lime trees arching overhead. There would be a mountain of washing as a result of this outing. The mud was six inches deep at the gate to the fair. The farmer beamed at the sight of so many new customers.

'Seventy farthings,' he said in glee, counting Felix and Robin as part of the party.

Phoebe kept watch over Clover as the little girl produced the golden half-guinea, and in turn she was aware of Felix watching her. How she wished that he was short, ugly and completely unthreatening as she attempted to keep track of the coins. He was ruining her concentration, but surely . . .

'I think you'll find that Clover requires another shilling if the change is to be exact,' she suggested.

'Sorry, Miss Allen,' said the farmer, fumbling with his great sack of farthings and giving the correct change.

Clover carefully doled out tiny copper coins to all her companions, including Felix and Robin.

'Each person can have two treats. I'm going to ride on the ups-and-downs and have some gilt-covered gingerbread to eat,' she told them.

The smell of crushed grass and the oyster and sausage stall was strong in the air. The excitement of the fair got into your blood. Suddenly forgetting their shyness, the girls flocked around Felix and Robin, excitedly calling about hot pies and the Punch and Judy show and a whole troupe of cunning little dogs.

As soon as they had their allowances, the children scattered like sparrows. Phoebe made no attempt to call them back. She could not compete with excitements such as a knife-swallower and a performing bear.

Miss Pennyfeather hiccupped genteelly.

'Shall we wait for the girls at the refreshment stall?'

Robin glanced at Felix, nodded as if he'd received an order, and then gallantly offered Miss Pennyfeather his arm.

'Might I escort you?'

Phoebe was alone with Felix. Her gaze lifted to his face as if pulled there on a silent command. Her breathing constricted. He was so tall and straight and beautifully masculine. She prayed her face didn't look as pink as it felt. He held out an arm with an encouraging smile.

'Would you care to accompany me?'

What choice did she have?

His arm was strong, of course, and it was a thrilling pleasure to be strolling over the crushed grass next to him, although Phoebe felt self-conscious by his side. She wanted to say something to make the moment ordinary, but she couldn't think of a thing. They walked in silence.

A booth owner came out and lit two flares, making the evening sky look navy against the blaze of orange and yellow flames. She was very aware of the man beside her. Why didn't he say something? Was he feeling the same tension that she was?

At last Felix stirred beside her.

'Isn't that one of your charges?' he asked, pointing at a six-year-old girl sobbing her heart out next to the pie stall.

'Maisie Banks!' cried Phoebe, flying to the rescue. 'What's the matter?'

'A big boy knocked me over!' Maisie sobbed. 'I dropped my money in the mud.'

Phoebe forgot Felix while she was mopping and hugging and finding some new coins, but when a happily restored Maisie skipped away, she straightened up and turned around to find him watching her with thoughtful green eyes.

'You are kind to those little girls.'

'And why should I not be?' she laughed.

'Is it not a bore, looking after so many people?'

'I like to be useful. I like to be needed.'

'Do you never wish that you had time for yourself?'

'Perhaps more time to read and play the piano; that, I own, would be my dream. But it's not of the least use hankering for what cannot be.'

He looked at her for so long that her

mouth went dry. That queer, inhibiting tension returned. What was it about this man's company that made her feel so wooden? She could talk all the day long to anyone else. She was glad when a smoky golden spicy fragrance floated along the air, tapping her on the nose to announce its presence. She took in a deep breath. It smelt delicious.

'What is that amazing smell?' she asked.

Felix lifted his nose and sniffed.

'Mulled wine,' he decided. 'It does smell magical.'

On their left was a fire of logs sending plumes of smoke and spirals of sparks flying up into the night. Over it was set a black iron trivet, and from that hung a black iron cauldron. Wisps of sweet-smelling steam rose from the pot. A crone in a sacking apron waved a wooden spoon at them.

'That's right, my darlings! Come along and taste Old Meg's punch.' Firelight flickered on her face, making her a creature of shadows as she chanted. 'What will be is written in the stars. Come drink my star juice and see what your fortunes will be.'

'What does she mean?' Phoebe asked, enthralled, drifting closer.

'It's just patter,' Felix answered. 'Would you like your fortune telling?'

Old Meg cackled.

'I don't tell fortunes, but brew them, and I see love for you two. Drink my magic drink, and you'll see.'

The smell was stronger, wilder, and even sweeter as they drew near. Meg had filled two pewter mugs before Phoebe could say, 'Those cups cannot be clean.'

Meg cackled again.

'My magic drink never hurt anyone, dear.'

'Well, I suppose if I survived Spain,' Felix mused, handing over a generous payment.

Phoebe took a tiny, cautious sip, but the red drink was nectar. It was hot, crimson, full-blooded as dragon's blood and fragrant with orange spices. It was a magic fluid calculated to make a woman forget the danger of a man's smile. The rest of the brew flowed down her throat in an easy, invigorating stream. Her odd shyness fell away to be replaced by wild exhilaration. An elephant padded past them, gorgeous in a red howdah. Phoebe gave an unself-conscious skip.

'My word! This is fun! I haven't been to a fair in years. Not since I was a little girl.'

His answering smile turned her to jelly. They walked on, but now she felt happy and relaxed. Music blared as they passed a splendid round-a-bout, all golden horses and crimson cockerels. The magic of the night was infecting her, running in her veins and making her toes tap to the tunes that whirled around them. Now she chatted freely as they wandered around the booths. She hummed gaily as they examined the sheep and guessed the weight of the fat lamb.

'Do you always sing when you are

happy?' Felix asked her.

She looked at him, aware of the tousle of his chestnut hair, the shadow of a beard forming on his chin. She couldn't help feeling attracted to him, even though she knew she was a fool to feel it. But tonight was so special that care had flown out of the window.

Next they stopped by the ride-a-bull ring. Phoebe covered her eyes in horror as a farmer's son was bucked off a massive curly-horned black bull and flung to the ground, but when he scrambled to his feet unharmed and jumped over the fence to safety with the bull snorting behind him, she let out a merry peal of laughter.

'Why do men have to prove themselves?' she asked her companion.

Felix had just been thinking how much he was coming to like her and had decided she would do for his mother. How many females would have soured in the face of the hard life that was so patently hers? Yet the kindness she showed to her small charges, who clearly adored her, was delightful. She worked with an innocent gusto that was most attractive. Her shining eyes as she took in the fair made him wonder how many treats she had in her life. Not many, he'd be bound.

And then she laughed. Her laugh was fine, open, infectious, full of sunshine, but what lady laughed aloud? He was in a fair way to falling for her charms, but what would his mother think?

Sensing his mood, she walked silently next to him. Another point in her favour, Felix mused. She could be silent, and she must have a sensitive heart to know that he wished to be quiet.

At the edge of the field was a tall hedge with an oak wood behind it. The moon was low on the horizon, silver against the summer sky.

Felix suddenly realised that he was happy. He wondered why his dark feelings had lifted. Maybe Phoebe's sunny approach to life was infectious?

And with that his mind was made up.

He turned to face Phoebe, meaning to issue the invitation, but she was standing a little closer to him than he had expected, with her heart-shaped face turned towards him, and her lovely clear gaze looking directly at him. She smelled faintly and deliciously of roses.

'Miss Allen,' he began.

'Yes?' she breathed softly.

Phoebe was astounded when his fingers gently touched under her chin, holding it captive, lifting it towards him, using it to control the rest of her face. She felt a catch at her heart. He bent his head, and then his lips touched hers in the gentlest brushing kiss. The sensation was so light, so new, so pleasurable, that she gasped.

She was kissing a man!

Phoebe's heart walloped against her ribs and she tore her lips away and fell back in shock. Run away! she told herself, but her body was frozen. Only her heart slammed in her chest.

His hands fell to his side, and he did not stir again. His green eyes were distant in the cool light of the moon, yet oddly intimate. She could see darker shards shining in the green of the iris, and those dark shards smouldered and shone. Phoebe felt the heat of that smouldering. It flashed in her veins like magic.

Ah, there was too much magic in the air between them. What was a girl to do? She had to draw on all her strength of character and remind herself how dangerous such magic could be. The attraction she felt may be magic, but it was also physical, and the physical she would and could overcome.

She wrenched herself away and ran. There is no place for moonlight kisses and magic in my life, she thought, sadly. Part of her hated to leave him, but then common sense came to her aid. She felt enchantment, but she also knew it was a fairy-tale. For one night only she, the beggar maid, was walking out with Prince Charming in all his finery. She wasn't running from an important relationship. How could he be thinking of anything other than a few moments of pleasure?

She heard footsteps thudding on the ground after her.

'Miss Allen?'

The snappy little remark she had prepared flew out of her mind when she met his eyes. For a moment she thought that Mr Chando was as bewildered as she was. His green eyes begged her to say something that explained the moment that had just passed between them. And then she reminded herself that he was in the wrong. He should not have kissed her. It was up to him to restore harmony, if it could be done after such an intense moment.

He put out a hand, as if in appeal, but Phoebe drew back. Still, she had lost the urge to bark at him.

'The orphans will be waiting,' she said gently. 'We go home at ten o'clock.'

She whirled and ran lightly across the grass. The sweet chimes of the church clock floated across the field, making her feel like Cinderella. The final silvery note rang just as she reached the gate, and there was Farmer Green in his hay wagon, stopping his white horse by the gate.

'Now then, Miss Phoebe, I told you I'd be on time, didn't I?'

'Thank you, Mr Green. I'll collect up the girls as soon as I can.'

'No hurry,' said that amiable man, jumping out of his seat and coming to the head of his horse.

Phoebe and Kitty ran about the fair collecting their charges. She had a feeling between her shoulder blades that suggested Felix was watching her, and just as she completed her head count, she felt his presence beside her. She wanted to feel calm, but quivers started up inside her because of his closeness.

'I've lost Miss Pennyfeather,' she said, hoping only she could hear the unnatural sound in her voice.

'Here she is now,' he replied.

Phoebe understood the smile in his voice when she saw Robin and Miss

Pennyfeather arm in arm, tottering towards them. Both of them were pink and beaming.

'Can you believe that I never tasted port and lemon before?' Robin said. 'It's a splendid drink and we've had a splendid time, haven't we, Miss P?'

Phoebe turned to the wooden hay wagon, but a masculine voice halted her.

'Wait, Miss Allen.'

What was it about Felix that made her act like a fool? She couldn't bear to talk to him. Panicked, she vaulted into the hay wagon.

'Drive on!' she called.

But Farmer Green lounged by the head of his horse, grinning. It took her a second to realise what, or rather who, had got into the man. Something told her it would be of no use to argue.

'Sit by us, Miss Phoebe!' begged the girls.

She put an arm around a child on either side of her, feeling oddly as if the warm bodies were protecting her rather than the other way around.

All the time, she knew he was waiting, standing by the side of the wagon, and at last she looked at him. He was smiling, and the moon was so bright you could see the green of his eyes.

'You look like a mother hen with all her chicks under her wings,' Felix said.

His quiet, intimate tone suggested a new bond had formed between them. Phoebe searched his eyes, looking for amusement, to see if he was taunting her, and yes, hidden in the luminous green depths, there was a flicker of amusement, but it was a gentle joy. She felt that he was laughing with her rather than at her. She smiled. She couldn't help it. Something had definitely changed between them. A barrier was down.

He touched the brim of his hat.

'I shall wait upon you tomorrow.'

Felix nodded to Farmer Green who touched his cap and clicked to his horse. The wagon stuck in the mud and then jolted on its way. Phoebe looked back. Felix's tall straight figure joined Robin's smaller one, and then the two men melted into the moonlight and darkness.

4

The working day at Miss Pennyfeather's began long before six, and by ten o'clock the next morning, Phoebe was exhausted. She knew the seminary was busy, but she'd never realised how many people came calling every day. The knocker never stopped its rat-a-tat-tat. In the last hour, the door had been assaulted by the butcher's boy, the baker, the cobbler, the curate with some pamphlets, a firewood delivery, a gipsy selling pegs, the greengrocer, the coalman and a girl from the milliner's with a new hat for Miss Pennyfeather.

The sound of every footstep outside, and every shadow at the window made Phoebe jump and sent shivers down her spine. You're a fool, she scolded herself. He won't come! You are an idiot to be waiting for him. But she couldn't help it. I have to stop, she thought desperately. I'm going to give myself a headache, and that's a luxury I can't afford!

She knew that the linen would need sorting because it always did, and the linen cupboard was in the heart of the house, right at the back of the servants' stairs and out of earshot of the door. She took herself off to the shelf-lined room and sorted, stacked and counted with gusto.

The room smelt of last year's lavender. It was high time to take the girls to the garden to harvest this year's blooms and then show them how to stitch lavender bags. It was one of her favourite chores, yet Phoebe felt savagely depressed. This would be the third year she'd spent at the seminary, the third time she'd seen lavender bloom in the kitchen garden. She had a sense that life was passing her by.

'Miss Phoebe!' a voice screamed from the stair well. 'Miss Phoebe! You'll never guess!'

Phoebe popped her head out of the cupboard.

'Quietly, Susie. Take a deep breath.'

The little maid's eyes were like saucers.

'He's here! Betsy went and got the missus out of bed and took her to the parlour, only it's not Miss Pennyfeather he wants — it's you!'

'He' was so much in her mind that Phoebe knew exactly who must be waiting in Miss Pennyfeather's parlour below, but she managed to say calmly: 'It's nothing to be so excited about.'

But her heart was beating so hard that it nearly choked her as she hurried down the white-painted corridors, fighting a ridiculous impulse to tear off her apron and smooth down her hair. The simple task of opening the door and walking into Miss Pennyfeather's best parlour had never seemed so fraught.

The fire was out and the room was cool, shadowy and dim. One figure sat on the brocade sofa, another on a gilt chair. It was so silent Phoebe could hear the slow sonorous tick of the grandfather clock. She crossed the room and flung up the blinds.

The light fell on a tall, dark and undeniably handsome figure. She was bowled over by the impression he made. Surely he hadn't been dressed so magnificently yesterday? Phoebe's gaze raced up his body, taking in the splendour of shining black boots, tight-fitting breeches, a snowy waterfall of immaculate linen and the capes of a well-tailored coat that showed off, oh gosh, the broadest of shoulders.

His impact wouldn't have been so faint-making if he'd looked stuffy or overdressed, but he didn't. He just looked comfortable. And on second glace, Phoebe could see that his clothes fit him comfortably, conforming snugly to his hard male body, yet allowing for the ease of movement that was so much a part of him. Dressed this way, he was more devastating than ever. He was causing havoc with Phoebe's racing pulse! She looked hard at the polished stone flags of the floor and willed her confusion to subside.

'I'll leave you,' Miss Pennyfeather moaned in feeble tones.

'Please don't!' Phoebe cried, still not looking up.

But she smelled gin and peppermint wafting by, and the click of the door informed her that her employer had left the room.

Phoebe's breathing came a little faster. She suddenly wanted her papa. She needed his protection, his calming presence. She needed to share the perplexing problem of the way this man made her feel with someone who cared. Thinking of her father had brought tears to her eyes. She caught her breath. She was on her own, and she would have to deal with Felix Chando, and the way he made her feel. She was afraid that he was looking at her; she was wishing that he wouldn't; she was wondering what on earth he was doing here and most of all she wanted to know why, oh why, it was so impossible to control the trembling of her knees.

'If you were to sit . . . ' his deep voice suggested, 'I have an important matter to discuss with you.'

His exquisitely male tone of voice sounded deep and rich in the small plain room.

Phoebe sank onto one of the oak chairs. She heard wood scrape on the floor as he pulled out another chair and sat next to her at the table. She looked away from him, but she could feel the heat of his gaze on her face.

'First, I must tell you that I am not who I initially presented myself to be.'

Phoebe's eyes flew open and she looked at him in amazement. A hint of uneasiness shaded the green eyes. She guessed this was a man who normally had little to do with subterfuge.

'You're not?' she gasped, idiotically. 'You're not Felix Chando?'

He straightened his shoulders and cleared his throat.

'No, well, yes, that is, in part. My

name in full is Felix George Edmund Henry, and I am the Earl of Chando.'

Phoebe knew she was goggling, but she couldn't help it. It was unbelievable, but there was the magnificence of the man to prove that he was an aristocrat, and somehow the fact that he looked faintly embarrassed by what he said made it seem true.

Feeling cross because she hated to be bewildered and was used to being in charge, Phoebe swallowed, took a breath and mustered her wits about her.

'But what is an earl doing in a ladies' seminary?'

'I am looking for Miss Phoebe Allen.'

'Me,' she gasped astounded. 'Why?'

'My Aunt Eugenie is not very well and so my mother went to visit her.'

The pause that followed seemed to go on for ever, which was just what Phoebe wanted. She could feel her system settling, cooling, and returning to her control, but then she looked up and met his green eyes and that unmistakable magic flashed around her system again. It made it hard to concentrate, but she was pretty sure he hadn't explained himself properly!

'Sir, I must beg you to be clear.'

'Aunt Eugenie is my mother's sister.'

'And your mother is . . . '

'Georgiana, Dowager Countess of Chando. She married my father, of course, and her sister, Eugenie, married George Thorpe.'

Phoebe gazed at the deep green of his eyes, knowing that the name of Thorpe rang a faint bell, but for the life of her unable to make the connection. Her brain did not seem to be working. It was distracted, busy, trying to work out why something hot and disturbing seemed to glitter in the air every time she and this handsome earl looked at one another.

'Thorpe,' she said as she suddenly realised the connection. 'My mother's maiden name was Thorpe, but my mother's relatives cast her off.'

'Until recently the family thought

that your mother, Arabella Thorpe as she was, died without issue. My Aunt Eugenie was putting her affairs in order when she discovered the truth.'

'I am confused. Eugenie is not a relative by blood?'

'The blood connection to you is through her husband, George Thorpe, but she has strong family feelings and a tender heart.'

'She wishes to heal the breach? I can assure you, sir, my father never spoke of it. Please tell Eugenie, and your mother, not to worry. All was forgiven many years ago and it is quite forgotten.'

He smiled.

'You are so quick to forgive; so generous.'

One of his hands stretched out and covered hers. She didn't pull away. His touch was pleasurable. Phoebe looked down at their hands, at the way his large one covered her small one. There was something so natural, so friendly about the way they were touching.

'Then we are related,' she said in a small voice.

'Distantly,' he said in his deep voice. 'And that brings me to the second part of my mission. My mother's health is not good. She finds our long dark winters somewhat lonely. She asks if you would like to stay with her as a companion.'

Phoebe snatched back her hand.

'Oh no! I'd rather dig ditches.'

Thunder instantly crossed his brow.

'Why, pray?' he drawled.

Phoebe realised that he'd taken deep offence.

'Sir, I apologise if I seemed rude. I spoke before I thought — '

'Ladies think before they speak!' he snapped.

'I am a school teacher, not a lady,' she fired, and then she realised why he was angry. 'Please, my response is in no way personal. I do not know your mother! But consider my position. My life at the school is like an anchor. I feel secure here.'

'You would be secure at Elwood,' he said in a slightly softer tone. 'We live on the coast, near Lancaster. It is a beautiful part of the country. The old castle burned to the ground and the house is small and modern. You will find it comfortable.'

'Sir, it sounds charming, but I cannot visit.'

His dark brows snapped together.

'No? You prefer a life of drudgery at this bizarre establishment?'

'The school is humble, it is true, but I am secure in my position and here I am useful.'

'I do not understand how you could prefer to be useful to a Miss Pennyfeather rather than my mother!' Anger and disappointment made his voice cruel. 'Have you thought of the future? Is your best friend and companion to be a square black bottle?'

Phoebe instantly picked up the gauntlet.

'It is character that determines the end of one's days, just as surely as it determines the beginning.'

He regarded her steadily with those green eyes, the colour dark and shadowed today. It was impossible to read his thoughts. He stirred, and then said more gently,

'Forgive me. I was motivated by affection for my mother.'

She liked him better for his apology. Was there any chance she could make him understand?

'I have a horror of becoming dependent. Being a companion would be like being a prisoner.'

'You could leave Elwood at any time.'

'As a rich man, you have the power and the means to travel as you wish. If I were to leave my place here, and then not be happy at your house, I would not be able to escape so easily.'

She felt her heart beating in the seconds that followed. His gaze grew bright, like a star, and he drew in a breath and leaned forward.

'I have not yet told you. Aunt Eugenie perhaps does not know how expensive life is today, but she was troubled by the idea that you may be in difficult circumstance, and she has settled the trifling sum of five hundred guineas a year upon you.'

'Five hundred guineas,' Phoebe repeated slowly.

'It is not much . . . '

His voice seemed to come from very far away. She heard a deep man-rumble, but she couldn't make out the sense of his words as he went on speaking. She nodded at intervals and prayed that he'd keep talking while she used the time to recover. And he did. He carried on explaining that his man of business was with him; that he had such a sum in his possession; that he was authorised to hand it over now; that further instalments of a hundred and twenty five guineas would follow, every quarter day, regular as the seasons, every season, every year until she died.

It was a fortune!

She was a free woman!

In the blink of an eye, with a few words from a deep voice, Phoebe was liberated from the cares of tactfully managing, washing, feeding and generally looking after sixty-seven people and set free to live in a paradise where she might have a little garden and read as much as she chose.

'Miss Allen?' he was questioning. 'Miss Allen, are you quite well?'

She lifted her gaze to his face, meeting his green eyes. His appearance was already burned into her being, raising her pulse, her heat, her awareness of herself as a woman. That alone was significant enough, but on top of that, like a crashing wave, came the loosening of her chains. Phoebe's feelings were vast, tumultuous, and threatening to break free. She could only hope that she could control them while he was still in the room.

'Miss Allen?' he said again. 'It's not a large sum, but . . . '

'Not much, you say? It's a fortune! Why, I will be independent.'

He inclined his head gravely.

'Then I am glad to be the bearer of welcome news.'

Phoebe stared at him, trembling.

'I could have a piano!'

And with that she burst into tears.

With a tender care that was in complete contrast to the sharp way he'd spoken to her earlier, Felix placed his hands at the back of her waist and drew her onto his lap as he sat again. Phoebe felt shocked, but then she remembered that they were related, and allowed herself to melt into his embrace. They fitted perfectly. She felt comforted, she felt protected, and she felt whole. Her tears faded. And then she remembered how distantly they were related and she took her head out of the niche it had found in his shoulder and felt shy. He threaded his fingers through hers and held her tight. For a moment, her grey eyes met his green eyes. Phoebe took a gasping breath.

'I'm sorry.'

She hoped her face wasn't telling too

much of a story. She knew her eyes would be bright with tears, she could feel that her cheeks were pink with embarrassment, and her lips, oh dear, her lips were remembering the magic of his kiss only yesterday. All by themselves, they had parted, and now they were inviting, even hopeful.

She wriggled off his knee and moved away from his embrace on shaking knees. She missed the heat of his body at once. Part of her felt as if she had escaped from a dangerous wild beast, the other as if she'd lost her best friend.

Felix sat quietly and he tactfully looked out of the nearest diamond-paned window while she applied a white linen handkerchief to blotting up her tears. Finally she was composed enough to explain.

'I haven't cried since Papa died.'

His green eyes were gentle.

'I am sorry for your loss.'

'I loved my papa dearly.'

'You are lucky!'

The words came with such feeling

that her gaze flew to his face, startled. His expression was open, his eyes undefended. His eyes were dark as he spoke.

'I was glad when my own father died.'

'That is sad, indeed.'

For a long minute he studied her face, and then his features stiffened. A line of ice formed behind the green eyes, shutting his thoughts away from her.

Phoebe knew that withdrawal was a natural reaction for a man who felt he had exposed too much emotion, but she still felt a catch at her throat as he shut her out of his heart. He stood up and picked up his hat from the table.

'Thank you for bringing the news,' she said, quickly, breathlessly, longing for something, but not knowing what.

He was polite, a figure made of ice with polished manners and an exquisite bow.

'It was my pleasure to be of service to you, Miss Allen.'

A sudden smile lit his face and restored humanity to his eyes.

'There are certain moments of our encounter that I shall remember forever. I am only sorry that I shall have to disappoint my mama by saying that you will not visit her.'

Now Phoebe knew what she was waiting for.

'I should like very much to visit your mother.'

He shook his head just the slightest, baffled fraction.

'But you refused the invitation, did you not?'

'That was when I was poor. Now that I'm a lady of means, I am free to do as I choose, and I should love to meet your mother.'

5

Only a day later, Phoebe found herself travelling by mail coach to the first town on the way north to Elwood. The coach hurtled through the muddy lanes, scattering sheep as it went.

'What an exciting way to travel!' Kitty cried.

'Umm,' Phoebe said, holding her stomach.

She felt as green as a cabbage by the time they arrived at Kibbton early that evening. She had to sit on a stone mounting block with a glass of water, but fresh air soon put her right.

Kibbton looked like a jolly and prosperous town. On the left was a triangular green that smelt of hay and the White Hart Inn rose serenely out of some lovely gardens. A sweeping stone arch led into a coaching yard. Felix went straight to one of the stables and began petting a magnificent black stallion.

Phoebe saw a stable man pelting out of the stables and into the back door of the hotel. She could hear him shouting. 'The Earl of Chando is here!'

The innkeeper, his wife, the head-waiter and an inordinate number of underlings belted into the yard and began bowing low. Phoebe was flabbergasted when she realised that most of the servants worked for Felix. Despite his air of consequence and his stunning tailoring, despite knowing that Felix considered a fortune such as five hundred guineas a year a small sum, it was still not until this moment that Phoebe truly understood the elevated status of her new relative.

She felt dizzy with the noise and the tumult and the unaccustomed number of faces, many of them, she suddenly noticed, casting curious glances at her. Phoebe looked up at Felix. She felt her heart catch as he met her eyes.

She blushed and murmured, 'I do

not think I would have been brave enough to agree to accompany you, if I had realised how truly splendid you are!'

'I'm glad you did,' he said, his green eyes glittering.

There was masculine certainty in the way he was looking down at her, and although the way he had spoken was casual enough, there was nothing casual about his look. It was intense in a way that threatened to melt her heart. Phoebe quickly turned away and looked around her for Kitty.

'Kitty?' she called.

Phoebe kept her back to Felix, but she knew exactly, to an inch, where he was standing behind her. She also knew that he was looking at her. She was ridiculously relieved when the little maid scurried out of the crowd to stand next to her. Kitty's eyes were as round as horn buttons.

'Have you seen that gold coach?' she whispered. 'We're going in it tomorrow! It's got red velvet seats.'

Robin strode out of the inn entrance. His expression wasn't as jolly as usual.

'Here's a bally nuisance. There isn't an extra room to be had!'

Felix enquired turned to an underling.

'Do we not have a suite reserved here, Dalton?'

His valet, Dalton, crimsoned.

'There is an acute shortage of accommodation.'

The innkeeper stepped forward to apologise.

'We've never been so full in my life. Black Peter's to be hung tomorrow, and nobody wants to miss the fun. I was never thinking of you needing an extra room because you was fetching — '

His curious gaze swung to Phoebe, who suddenly became acutely aware of the grey plainness of her orphanage gown.

'My cousin,' Felix said, and this time the smile had disappeared and his voice was a snap.

Dalton began hastily, 'We shall pay

someone to move — '

'Thank you, Dalton. I leave the arrangements to you.'

Visibly losing interest, Felix turned away.

Phoebe said, more quickly than she would have done if she had been perfectly calm, 'Kitty and I can sleep anywhere. We don't need a room all to ourselves.'

Felix swung back and seemed to study her so deeply that she suffered an inner jolt. His gaze never left her face, again taking in so much more than mere features. He seemed to read what her life had been, and he looked angry.

'Never say that!' he told her. 'Never say that you can sleep anywhere or put up with anything! You deserve the best.'

Phoebe melted inside and followed him into the inn as docilely as a little lamb. It was such heaven to have someone looking out for her! She couldn't believe how kind he was, more, how tender he was being to her. She warned herself not to read too much into his behaviour. She was a fool to think that he might be beginning to care for her. He was just being Felix: strong, kind, always looking out for others.

Standing in the stone-flagged entrance hall was a stout lady arguing with Dalton. Felix walked straight past their spirited conversation, but Phoebe heard the woman protesting.

'But we spoke for our room the second they pronounced the sentence and we knew there'd be a hanging. My maid ran straight out of the courtroom to arrange matters.'

Phoebe touched Felix's arm.

'Can it be right for us to spoil that lady's plans and her pleasure?'

Felix gave her a long, surprised look. And then he smiled.

'Forget it. Dalton will arrange everything.'

The surety of his response made her feel off balance, but Phoebe was never one to shirk a battle.

'I think we should make sure she is

happy,' she declared.

Felix felt angry as he met her clear expectant eyes. How dare she doubt his judgement!

'I told you to forget the matter,' he snapped.

Her eyes went very wide and hurt bloomed in the grey depths. She turned her head and looked away. Felix's stomach twisted. What had made him attack her so meanly? Well, she'd get back at him. Words were a woman's weapon. She'd be gathering herself for retaliation, and if she nagged him he'd know that she was a shrew as well as a prig. But Phoebe's silence was thunderous. Felix felt sick. He hadn't meant to hurt her. Was she crying? The brim of her bonnet hid most of her face, but when he looked at the furious angle of her chin, he realised that tears didn't enter into her feelings. She was livid. The silence between them seemed to vibrate with her anger.

Well he was angry, too. Felix glared at her small figure. He'd made a huge mistake fetching such an irritating woman to Elwood. What if she started trying to lecture and improve his mother? He put a hand on her arm.

'Come along,' he ordered.

Something about the way he was looking at her made her feel in the wrong, but she ignored her uncomfortable feelings, broke free from his grasp and closed the short distance between her and the stout lady.

'Excuse me, ma'am,' she said. 'I think we may be causing you too much inconvenience.'

But the stout lady chuckled and folded a wodge of crackling bank notes, stuffing them into the folds of the large crimson umbrella she was carrying.

'Me and Mr Hoity Toity here have come to an arrangement. I'll do very nicely in the innkeeper's wife's bed.'

Felix walked up to Phoebe and offered her his arm. A smile flickered around his lips. She flushed as she took his arm and walked into the dining parlour. She knew little of men and it was hard to interpret his expression. Thank goodness Robin was dining with them. He kept the conversation light as they ate cold beef and then apple pie.

Later that night she stretched out luxuriously in the bed, which was an oak four-poster with a splendid feather mattress. Felix was always kind to her, so why did she find him so unnerving? Surely she had been right to consider that poor woman's welfare? Yes, and Felix had been right that Dalton would arrange everything so that everyone was happy.

We were both right, Phoebe thought, smiling. Sensibly she stopped puzzling her head, snuggled up in the feather pillows and drifted off to sleep.

* * *

'Good morning, cousin.'

Felix's heart lifted when he heard the rustle of female skirts and smelled the delicious scent of roses. He turned to greet Phoebe, admiring her clear colouring and thinking that it was curious that her face looked more beautiful above her simple grey dress than it would have done over a trimmed and coloured gown.

Her bright grey eyes were busy absorbing the men scurrying around the stable making ready the coach and horses.

'You are like a comet with a trail of retainers,' she mused.

As Phoebe's grey eyes smiled and dared him to comment, Felix quelled the urge to point out that in Spain he'd been perfectly comfortable with the services of a single batman and was delighted to see the orphanage girl trailing reluctantly towards them.

'Your maid adds to the numbers,' he pointed out triumphantly.

Phoebe acknowledged his riposte with a smile that made his heart bound, but she immediately turned her attention to the maid's unhappy face.

'Are you feeling quite well, Kitty?'

'Yes, miss,' Kitty replied, but a few

minutes after they all squeezed into the coach and settled into the red velvet seats, she burst into tears.

Phoebe put an arm around Kitty.

'Is it the toothache?'

Kitty shook her head, tears rolling down her face.

Felix watched Phoebe tending to her maid and decided that a motherly air suited her. After prolonged coaxing, Kitty finally whispered a few words, and then Phoebe lifted a face full of mingled disapproval and laughter.

'What's the problem?' Felix asked, admiring the way Phoebe's black lashes heightened the brightness of her grey eyes.

'She's sorry not to see Black Peter hang!'

Felix never lost control. He'd spent a lifetime training himself to have absolute command over his feelings because he never, never, never wanted to behave like his wild and selfish father. Yet the mixture of expressions on Phoebe's face made him want to laugh out loud. If he looked at her again, he'd explode with mirth. He looked very hard out of the opposite window. The coach was rumbling and jolting over a moor. Felix signalled the head coachman to stop.

'I shall ride my horse,' he announced.

The coach jolted to a halt and everyone got out to stretch their legs.

Felix mounted his ebony charger and Kamil snorted and bucked, sending water splashing as his hooves kicked up spray from a silver puddle. Far from reining the horse in, Felix turned its head toward the moor and gave the command to go faster. The black stallion gave a happy leap and pelted for the top of the hill. Felix let the horse gallop freely until he reached the top of the hill. There he reined in his horse. The fresh air was invigorating and Kamil's paces felt like silk after the shaking of the coach, but his mind hadn't settled at all. What was it about Phoebe Allen that provoked him to emotions he rarely felt? She was dangerous. The less he had to do with her the better. He'd ride his horse for most of the journey.

Travelling by coach might be exciting, but it was not comfortable. Phoebe had her eyes closed and both hands on her stomach when she felt the vehicle slow, sway and finally stop for the gate into Elwood estate to be opened.

They rumbled through the gates and onto a long, long avenue which travelled straight as an arrow between acres of grass spangled with diamonds of rain. The road was lined with large tree stumps, the cut tops looking black in the drizzle. Robin shook his head sadly and commented to Felix: 'The avenue looks miserable with the great oaks gone. What a pity your father had all the trees felled.'

Felix's silence was thunderous.

'Of course, he had to pay his gambling debts,' Robin added quickly, and then he put a hand to his mouth as he realised how little he'd mended matters.

Felix had been in a dark mood since

the rain had forced him inside the coach. He seemed to have retreated behind walls of black iron. Phoebe felt that the space inside the coach was shrinking which was absurd; for feelings, no matter how strong cannot affect physical dimensions. Yet she would be devoutly thankful to escape the closed space, and she was glad to see the house approaching.

Elwood was set in a green hollow that was formed by the gently rising hills that rose all around. The house was built of warm yellow stone and stood three stories high. The proportions were serene and beautiful, and it was a prosperous, friendly building.

Their coach stopped on the gravel sweep before the house. Phoebe got out, thinking what a relief it was to have her feet on firm ground and to be breathing fresh air.

The surprise was that they were not alone. Already drawn up on the gravel was an elegant gilded coach.

Felix's face was perplexed.

'Who can this be?'

Luggage spilled off the roof of the coach and sat in disorganised piles on the gravel sweep. Staff fluttered like moths, but Phoebe realised that there was no order in their behaviour.

A stout footman with grey hair hurried up to their coach, panting. His brown eyes held distinct relief.

'Master Felix! We are in a pickle with Mr and Mrs Cooper and their daughter arriving unexpected. Mrs Cooper says that you are going to marry her daughter! It seems all wrong not to welcome them in, but you'd left no word to expect them, and Melville's not here, and well, we wasn't sure if it were right to let them in, the family not being what you might call a gentlefolk as is plain for anyone to see.'

Marry his daughter! Phoebe went cold all over and her ears buzzed. She cast a quick look at Felix's face. His eyes flashed frosty emerald. His expression looked stern and there was white skin around his lips.

He doesn't look like a man who is happy to meet his fiancée, Phoebe thought, and then she felt ashamed of herself. She knew she was clutching at straws. She was hoping for a mistake, to hear that he wasn't engaged after all. But when a young woman stepped around the corner of the fairy-tale coach, and the full splendour of her looks became apparent, every last vestige of hope was gone.

She was an exquisite little package with glossy blonde curls. Phoebe couldn't help but adore the blue travelling robe she was wearing. She was followed by her roly-poly father. His waistcoat was enough to make you blink, but a jolly smile lit up his face.

'Now then your lordship, you'll be surprised to see us here so quick, I'll be bound, but Thomas Cooper didn't get where he is today by letting the grass grow under his feet, and as soon as your man of business told me how the situation was, I set off for Elwood.'

Phoebe wanted to understand every

nuance of the situation. She knew she was staring, but she wasn't the only one. All the servants had stopped their scurrying and were drifting closer, listening as hard as they could.

Felix was polite, formal, and absolutely expressionless. She had no idea if he were pleased, amused or outraged. Phoebe watched as he lifted a quizzical eyebrow.

'And you say your wife is with you?'

'She's in the coach. Mother? Do come on, Mother!'

The roly-poly tradesman toddled to the coach and beckoned to his wife. The fairy-tale coach lurched on its springs. A wonderfully layered purple hoop skirt bent, billowed and finally popped out of the doorway of the carriage. Phoebe was astounded to hear an agonised yelping break out, and then she saw the woman in the crinoline was holding a shivering brown puppy by one ear. She saw Phoebe in her grey gown, and shoved the puppy at her.

'Take this beast out of my sight and

drown it. They are supposed to be all the fashion, but it's done nothing but yelp since we set off.'

Phoebe took the warm body and automatically supported it with her hands. The yelping stopped, but she could feel the little beast shaking.

'That's no way to treat a puppy!' she cried indignantly. 'How would you like it if a giant were to carry you around by one ear?'

All the watching servants took in a sharp breath, and then a frozen, paralysed silence fell as the woman turned to stare. Phoebe felt the full power of the outraged blue eyes that landed on her, and suddenly realised Mrs Cooper was not a woman to be trifled with. The cold gaze swept her up, and swept her down, and then Mrs Cooper turned to Felix.

'That's a funny way for a servant to speak to an earl's guests!'

A muscle flickered in Felix's cheek, but then, as if realising how ludicrous the situation was, he suddenly smiled.

'I must introduce you to my cousin, Miss Phoebe Allen. Miss Allen, I have the pleasure of introducing you to Mr Thomas Cooper, Mrs Thomas Cooper and Miss Cooper.'

Feeling like every kind of bumpkin in her plain grey gown, and somewhat hampered by the fact she was holding a puppy, Phoebe swept a curtsey.

So many faces were now turned to Phoebe that she was human enough to wish that she had a new dress for the occasion. She wanted to hide away from the stares. She bent her burning face over the puppy. It looked at her with pleading, humble eyes. It was a brown King Charles spaniel with the prettiest face.

The party moved towards the house. The servants shook themselves and worked with direction now that they knew the unexpected guests had permission to stay.

Phoebe, with Kitty stuck by her side like a faithful shadow, turned to the kind-looking footman.

'Could you help me find some food and water for this poor little dog?'

Elwood's stable yard boasted an air of calm order that was in complete contrast to the chaos in front of the house. Although grooms bustled around with nets of hay and buckets of water, settling the many horses that had just arrived, it was so peaceful you could hear white doves cooing on the stone tiles of the stable roofs.

The head groom, Spiller, appeared at once, took one look at the puppy, and sent a stable lad to fetch the huntsman.

'Warren looks after our dogs, Miss Allen,' he explained.

'Thank you,' said Phoebe, registering that he already knew who she was and probably a great deal else besides.

Spiller nodded at her, and a smile lit his hazel eyes.

'Do you ride a horse, Miss Allen?'

'I love horses, but I've never had the opportunity to ride.'

He smiled again, and gestured first at a row of stables each with a beautiful

Arab horse's head hanging over it, and then to a green paddock full of mares and foals.

'His lordship will show you around the stables if you ask him. Horse breeding is his passion.'

The huntsman arrived at a run. He cast a quick, curious glance at Phoebe from under his bushy brows before taking the puppy from her to examine it.

'There's nowt wrong that some grub and a rest won't fix.'

He whistled for a lad and told him to fetch some dog food.

'He's a darling,' Phoebe said, stroking the puppy. 'Do you think I might keep him, Warren?'

'Oh yes. I hear that woman told you clear enough to drown it.'

A cheerful scruffy boy scampered up to them with a puppy-sized portion of meat. The puppy wolfed its meal down. It then sat on its haunches and looked up at Phoebe with a distinct doggy smile in its melting brown eyes.

Warren nodded.

'He'll do. I'll have a dog basket taken to your room. And you send for me tomorrow and we'll start with his training, sooner the better, even for lap dogs.'

'I will. Thank you.'

The sound of a sweet-toned chime made Phoebe look at the stable clock. It was three o'clock! Felix — everyone — seemed to have forgotten about her and she had no idea what she was expected to do.

She tried not to mind being abandoned by Felix. It was only natural that, having had his undivided attention for so long, she should feel put out by his absence, but it was even more natural that a man with such a beautiful fiancée should forget his poor relation.

'What are we going to do, miss?' Kitty asked.

'Go into the house, I suppose,' Phoebe said, speaking bravely but wishing she was back at Miss Pennyfeather's.

6

The sheer size of the stone building intimidated her, she'd never been to such an enormous house before, but the oak doors were wide open, so Phoebe took a deep breath, crossed the threshold and stepped into the hall. It opened out like a massive cave. Chandeliers glittered from the ceiling, gilt-framed paintings adorned every inch of the walls, and statues and medieval weapons burst from every corner. Trunks, bundles and scattered hat boxes were dotted around the black and white marble floor.

'Well, miss,' Kitty tutted, clicking her tongue. 'You would have our guts for garters if we left a mess like this in the hall at Miss Pennyfeather's.'

'You may be right, Kitty, but let's not discuss it quite so loudly!'

A tall, thin female trotted down the

lovely oak steps that swept from the second floor and into the hall. Her prominent gooseberry-green eyes goggled coldly at Phoebe, and then at the puppy.

'You can't bring that beast in here!' the woman bleated. 'Take it out to the stables.'

Phoebe hesitated, unsure of her rights and her place in this very grand house, but here came Sam the footman, smiling benignly.

'Don't worry, Miss Belmont. The earl has given orders that his cousin should have a basket in her room for the little dog.'

One of his eyelids flickered down in a wink. Phoebe felt cheered, until she registered Miss Belmont's extreme reaction. The woman looked furious. Her gooseberry eyes were icy and her mouth was distorted with temper.

Phoebe was glad to hurry away with Sam up the sweeping oak staircase which was thickly hung with paintings. Yet for all the grandeur of the landscapes and portraits, she couldn't help but notice that the gilt frames were dull, and cobwebs were much in evidence.

Sam stopped at a wood-panelled door

'Here we are, Miss Allen. The yellow room has been prepared for you.'

Phoebe was amazed! Surely such a grand room couldn't be for her? It was enchanting, if radically full of furniture.

'Oh, Miss Phoebe!' Kitty breathed.

What could be seen of the walls for gilt looking-glasses, hunting scenes and pictures of Chandos from the Elizabethan era, was painted a sunny yellow. Three long, white-painted windows looked over green parkland. A fire blazed in the grate — a fire in August!

There were also two beds. The eyes of mistress and maid met in pure delight, remembering the sleeping arrangements at Miss Pennyfeather's. The beds had been comfortable enough, and the linen clean thanks to Phoebe's ministrations, but the girls slept top-and-tail at least six to a bed, and Phoebe was accustomed to feet on her pillow.

'White sheets!' breathed Kitty reverently, touching the pillow of the smaller bed.

A rat-a-tat-tat at the door heralded the entrance of a female with a quiet air of competence. She was dressed as a servant, but her lavender gown was of good material, her collar was real lace and she wore a fine cameo brooch.

'Well, it took me some time to find you, tucked away in the back of the house. I'm Jenny, the dowager countess's dresser, and she has sent me to help you get ready for tonight.' Keen, but friendly brown eyes swept up Phoebe's orphanage frock and back down again. 'Well, that dress won't do! What else have you brought with you, Miss Allen?'

'Two more exactly the same!' replied Phoebe, smarting slightly at Jenny's plain speaking. She thought gratefully of her fortune. Thank goodness she was independent. She need not worry if her clothes weren't good enough for company. 'Perhaps I could dine in my room tonight?'

Jenny's smile was kind, but firm.

'We can't have that. I'll be back shortly!'

Kitty and Phoebe unpacked their meagre belongings, stopping every few seconds to look at furniture, ornaments, pictures and knickknacks. There were enough cupboards, chests and drawers to store the entire belongings of sixty-eight people with space to spare and then some. Phoebe's two plain grey identical dresses looked tiny and lost hanging in one of the vast wardrobes.

'The little dog likes it here,' Kitty said, pointing to the brown shape curled on the hearthrug in front of the crackling fire. 'What are you going to call him?'

'He looks like a Pepe to me.'

Phoebe sank on to the rug next to the spaniel and cuddled the warm drowsy body. He licked her nose. The adoration that shone out of his brown eyes was a real comfort. At least she was good enough in Pepe's eyes!

A tap at the door heralded the return of the friendly Jenny, who was carrying a basket and had a delicious white froth of fabric over her arm.

'We thought this half slip worn over your grey . . . yes. Let me pull up the ribbons and tie them so! Well, that is better, I must say.'

She turned Phoebe to face the looking-glass. The addition of a foaming lace layer over the plain grey had transformed the orphanage gown.

Kitty sucked in her breath.

'Oh, miss! You look lovely.'

Jenny dove into her basket and got out a hairbrush. With a fascinated Kitty breathing down her neck and watching every move, she brushed Phoebe's hair until it gleamed, twisting it around her fingers to bring out the curl. Then she used pearl-studded blue velvet bands to lift and hold the hair arrangement.

Jenny clicked her tongue.

'That's the best I can do with no clothes to work with,' she sighed.

Phoebe examined her reflection in the looking glass. The soft lace overgown had transformed her appearance, but perhaps her hair was the biggest change. Her dark locks had been coaxed into curls and ringlets that lay on her shoulders and framed her face. The elegant style wonderfully softened her face and gave her an air of carefree youth. She felt blithe, a mood that she had not experienced, since, well, since Papa died.

Yet her expression was no longer that of a child. The pink lips that curved in the mirror looked subtly different because they had been kissed. Her cheeks glowed and her grey eyes sparked with adventure and excitement. Phoebe the child was gone. Phoebe the schoolmarm was slipping away. It was scary, but it was also exhilarating.

'Thank you, Jenny,' she said softly.

* * *

Never had such a bright waistcoat been seen in the library at Elwood. As Felix confronted the red-faced tradesman he found himself wondering why he'd allowed such vulgar people into his house. He hadn't wanted to confront the stranger with all the servants watching. Yet the man, far from appearing grateful to have been spared public humiliation, was sitting comfortably and beaming at him paternally.

'Now then, your lordship, I see you're surprised that I turned up so quick, but as I said before, Thomas Cooper never lets the grass grow under his feet.'

'I am at a loss to account for your presence at all.'

The man's very blue eyes opened wide.

'Your man of business thought of me the very moment you asked him to find a rich bride.' His chuckle was rich and robust. 'And I'm rich enough by all accounts. Aye, even rich enough to take on a great barn of a place like this what wants a good fettling. My Alicia is our only chick, my lord, and it'll all come to her when I'm gone. You'll not be selling your title cheap, that I do promise you.'

'I am not selling my title,' Felix protested.

Sharp blue eyes met his.

'That's not what your man said to me.'

Felix opened his mouth to protest, but before he could deny all responsibility in the matter, a cold icy hand reached out and gripped his stomach as he remembered.

'I did say, in a fit of depression, that my only recourse was to marry an heiress, but I never dreamed that Seward would take me seriously, still less that he would act on it. I certainly never commissioned him to find me a wife. I am sorry you have had a wasted journey,' he said, watching the tradesman warily.

The lurid waistcoat and the outward appearance of Mr Cooper made Felix expect an explosion of rage, but, although the blue eyes flashed cold steel, the man had admirable self-control. Felix couldn't help liking him when he smiled wryly.

'Your man got the wrong end of the stick and sent me on a wild goose chase, is that so, my lord? Well, there's no profit in bemoaning spilt milk. The question is, what am I to do about it?'

Again to his surprise, Felix felt no urge to squash the man's pretensions. 'You must stay overnight, of course,' Felix offered.

The tradesman flashed him a look.

'And the rest. Look at the matter from my point of view. Alicia and her mother have told all their friends that they are off to visit with a real live member of the aristocracy. How are they going to feel if they have to go home tomorrow and say that they was chucked out?'

Felix couldn't care less, but he wasn't a cruel man.

'Then you may stay one week.'

'And who knows, maybe you and my

Alicia will get on. She's a pretty little thing, that you can't deny.'

'I can assure you that my title is not for sale.'

'No, I can see that, my lord, but what if you was to take a fancy to the girl? Be different then, wouldn't it?'

'I shall never marry.'

Felix wondered what it was about this businessman that had prompted him to be so open. He was determined never to marry, but usually he didn't say so because he couldn't explain his reasons without speaking most disrespectfully of his father. He hoped the businessman would be content to leave the subject alone. He was clearly thinking the matter over.

Beneath Mr Cooper's tubby form and garish clothes was a keen intelligence and a force of character. He made no conventional protests, but he did not have the delicacy of character that would prevent him asking personal questions.

'I can see that you mean what you

say, my lord. Why are you so set against marriage?'

'I suppose you deserve the truth, and it will save you from wasting your time. I have no intention of carrying on the line.'

'What of the estate and your title?'

'It will go to a cousin.'

The blue eyes regarded him steadily. 'May I ask why?'

Felix hated talking about the man whose behaviour, or more accurately misbehaviour, had caused so many problems.

'I think my father's reputation tells its own story,' he said coldly.

He was afraid the man would ask more questions. Discussing the subject made him feel both ill and angry and he'd had enough but it seemed that Thomas Cooper had heard all about the old earl, and understood the situation perfectly.

'From what I hear, you are nothing like your father.'

'I have his blood but I will not yield

to it. I take every precaution. I keep myself under close control at all times.'

The blue eyes studied him, and then Mr Cooper nodded.

'Ask anyone and they'll tell you that Thomas Cooper is a good judge of men. You're worrying for nowt. You'll not go bad. I'd trust my little girl to you.'

Unexpectedly Felix found himself moved by the man's good opinion, so moved that he blurted out his greatest fear.

'What of the children? You can see in horses how a bad strain goes through the generations. I cannot take the risk.'

'Men are not animals, my lord.'

'I cannot take the risk,' Felix repeated. 'I have to look no further than my stables for an example. I have an Arab stallion called Shaitan. He's black as the devil he's named after and just as vicious. I should shoot him. Yet he's so fast and so beautiful that his foals are in high demand and I cannot bring myself to do it.'

'Why do you continue to breed from him?'

'Racehorses. You are not a racing man or you would know the bloodline. Shaitan has sired many a winner. Shaitan's foals all go out into the world with the warning that they should only be ridden by professionals.'

'What of your own horse? I hear that's an Arab?'

'It's true that Kamil is from Shaitan's line, but I never sell his foals as riding horses to other people.'

'Is Kamil vicious?'

'He seems gentle, but I take no risks. I would not trust any horse of Shaitan's blood. Beautiful as the horses are, blood always tells.'

Mr Cooper's blue eyes were kind as he got to his feet.

'There's no point us arguing. I can see that your mind is made up, my lord, so me and mine will stay the week out as we agreed and then we'll move on.'

Felix was feeling uncomfortable. Whatever had possessed him to confide his intimate secrets to one who wasn't a gentleman? He was worried enough to ask: 'You'll keep our conversation private?'

The hearty slap that landed on his back made him stagger.

'Your secrets are safe with me, my lord.'

And, against appearances, Felix believed the man.

'Please, call me Chando,' he invited as they left the room.

* * *

Phoebe guided a very nervous Kitty down to the servants' hall, and then promptly took a wrong turning herself. She walked through a long sunny gallery stuffed full with bizarre oddments of furniture such as suits of armour, rocking horses and a grand piano. When she came to a dusty looking glass with silver elephants around the frame, she couldn't resist stopping to look at her reflection. She had never looked better, but she felt terrible inside. Perhaps because of the portraits that hung on every available surface. Their eyes seemed to be watching her, judging her and wondering what a little school teacher was doing in such a majestic house.

At the end of the gallery a door opened onto a very grand flight of marble stairs. She went down them, hoping they would lead into the entrance hall. Instead she found herself in a small wooden hall with closed doors all around it. She paused, feeling like a rabbit caught in a trap. One of the doors clicked open, and a young footman in scarlet hurried out.

She opened her hands in a helpless gesture.

'I'm so sorry, but I am completely lost.'

A boyish smile lit his brown eyes.

'Follow me, Miss Allen.'

He chatted away as they walked, telling her that his name was Peter Fletcher, and that he loved his job and he couldn't abide cruelty to animals, but he clammed up and became a model of correctness as soon as they entered the vast hall with its chequered floor of black and white marble.

The footman led her around some carved screens and then past a spiky table made of elephant tusks to the far wall where a log fire blazed and crackled in a black iron grate.

Felix stood on the right, looking simply incredible in a dark evening coat with the most fabulous ruffles of white around his wrists and throat. Phoebe walked towards him as if she were hypnotised, but the footman discreetly touched her elbow. His light signal made her halt. Alicia, looking exquisite in a yellow dress with a delicious half train, and her mother, were standing next to Felix.

Trusting the footman's hint, she turned to the people who were gathered in a group on the left of the tall marble fire surround. She was shaking as she walked towards the fire.

Miss Belmont wore a white knitted cape with rather unfortunate bobbles that made her look more than ever like a sheep. She raised her cold gooseberry eyes.

'You are late, Miss Allen. We are all waiting for you.'

Phoebe curtseyed and murmured a dazed apology. She was thankful to see Robin turn to her with a jolly smile.

'You have not delayed us. May I introduce you to John Adam, the land agent, and Mr Connor, the curate?'

Phoebe curtseyed to everyone and hoped that she was saying the right things.

'Is the dowager countess here?' she asked.

Miss Belmont answered.

'She will join us for tea in the library. I don't like leaving her, but she always insists that I dine with the family.'

'Anything to get time alone without the Bleater!' Robin muttered naughtily in Phoebe's ear.

Most of Phoebe's attention was on

Felix. Heavens, but he looked gorgeous! His burnished mahogany hair fell at precisely the right angle, and he held himself with such poise, and yet, as she studied him, she realised that his face was darker than she'd ever seen it before. He looked troubled, yet he was chatting easily enough, and when dinner was announced he took Alicia's arm as gracefully as if he performed the action every day. Phoebe felt a stabbing pain in her heart as she watched. What a handsome couple they made.

Robin took Mrs Cooper's arm, and Miss Belmont walked off with the curate, leaving John Adam to take Phoebe's arm in a friendly fashion and escort her into the dining room.

A carved and gilded chair was pulled out for her, and she sank into the red velvet seat. The sheer acreage of table was daunting, not that you could see the surface for clutter. Every inch was littered with silver vases, cruet holders and whatnots that prevented the diners from seeing one another across the table. The air smelt fusty and she longed to throw open the windows.

She had a sudden vision of the merry meals at the seminary — the long scrubbed wooden table and the little hands reaching out for wholesome bowls of bread and milk or baked apples. Phoebe wished she were back there. But she was sitting in silence, and that would not do. They had never been grand at the vicarage, but her papa had insisted on good manners. She must ignore the familiar form of Robin on her right, and converse with the land agent on her left.

'It is a lovely evening, is not, sir?' she said.

John Adam turned towards Phoebe and she saw that he had an open expression and steady hazel eyes that she liked at once.

'We could certainly do with dry weather,' he returned. 'With all the rain we've had, the barley is at least two weeks behind.'

'Do you grow a good deal of barley?'

John Adam was more than happy to tell her about the business of the estate. He was soon talking about improvements they had made to a farm on the salt marshes.

'The drainage will have to pay for itself before we can tackle another farm, but it will. The Dutch engineering has doubled the number of sheep that land will support.'

Phoebe listened hard and ate little. Her nerves were affecting her stomach, and the stuffy atmosphere oppressed her senses, but what finished her appetite was the food. The first dish she tried was disgusting! It was some kind of greasy meat covered in rancid lard. The second dish she tried was worse. Trails of pink ran into the sauce and she saw lumps of undercooked liver. Abandoning the food with a shudder, she turned to Robin who was sitting on her right hand.

'Are you interested in land improvement?' she asked him.

'No, but I should be. I must learn to

play the farmer, I suppose, now that I've had to sell out.' He heaved a huge and heavy sigh at the prospect. 'Curse this stupid shoulder. It don't bother me one jot, you know, but the sawbones won't pass me as fit.'

'Won't you tell me a little about the war? I have never spoken to someone who was actually there. In England, Wellington was abused for exposing himself too much.'

Robin fired up at once.

'It's important for the commander-in-chief to show himself and inspect the troops in person!' he insisted.

Her companions were easier to manage than the food, Phoebe reflected, shuddering over the next course as a new set of dishes appeared on the table. She tried a chunk of stringy chicken that was in no way improved by its exotic garnish of fried cockscombs. It was lucky there was conversation to distract her, for she couldn't even bear to try dried-up lobster covered in blue cheese and cockles. Better, far better, to focus on Robin's tales of adventure.

'There must have been twenty thousand of them advancing on us, the best soldiers in France, led by the Emperor himself. The very ground was shaking! 'Hurrah!' Felix shouted to his men. 'They are within shot! Fire a volley!' And then, you know, he led the charge with fixed bayonets.'

'How grand of him!' Phoebe cried.

Alicia sat on the other side of the land agent and next to Felix. Felix was listening to a tirade of some kind from Mrs Cooper. His face was impassive. Alicia made no effort whatsoever to talk to John Adam. She seemed completely overawed by the situation, and looked for all the world like a frightened mouse sitting at a table full of hungry cats. When the signal for the ladies to withdraw was given, she scurried to the dining-room door and left in a scamper.

The library was as cluttered and disorganised as Phoebe had come to expect, but the rows of books gave it a friendly air. A profusion of maps, globes, books, pictures, statues, vases, trinkets and furniture met her curious gaze. Elwood House seemed to have the contents of three or even four households crammed into it, she mused.

A welcoming fire burned in a slightly smaller fireplace than the one in the hall. Near the fire sat the most beautiful dark-haired woman with a fine paisley shawl over her knees. She had clear green eyes exactly the same unusual colour and shape as Felix's.

Phoebe approached her shyly.

'I believe you may be my fairy godmother.'

The dowager countess put out a hand with a motherly gesture that went straight to Phoebe's lonely heart.

'My dear, I'm so glad to meet you.'

Her green eyes searched Phoebe's face. Like her son, she seemed to see below the features and into the soul of the person she was looking at. Then she smiled and gestured to Phoebe to sit down beside her.

'I wrote to Eugenie as soon as Felix

sent word that you were discovered. She was glad to hear that you are so very pretty.'

Had Felix truly sent such a flattering report? Or was it just the dowager countess's friendly way?

'I should like to say thank you to her.'

'There is no need. She is happy that you have been found and the ancient wrong righted.'

'Do please tell her that Papa never thought of it as a wrong, and he never taught me to think so.'

The dowager countess smiled.

'I shall write again to Eugenie and tell her how pleased I am that you have come to stay with me.'

Miss Belmont barged in.

'The fire is too hot, I'm convinced of it,' she bleated. 'We must take the greatest care of our invalid, mustn't we?'

She called for both of the footmen to move the chairs and to place screens. When they were finally re-settled the dowager countess turned to Phoebe with her friendly smile.

'How did you find the journey? I own that I never quite like crossing the sands at Morecambe.'

'Dearest Georgiana!' Miss Belmont bleated, leaning in between them. 'You look exhausted. You must not overtire yourself talking!'

Phoebe took the hint and stood up. Miss Belmont nipped smartly into the vacated chair. The dowager countess smiled and touched Phoebe's hand.

'Come and see me in the morning. I am tired now.'

'You were quite well before dinner,' Miss Belmont fussed. 'Perhaps your baked egg did not agree with you?'

'Adolphe thought that the lobster would suit me better,' the dowager countess said, and her stomach gave the most terrific gurgle, which everyone pretended not to hear.

Phoebe felt more at home. If there was one skill she did feel secure in, it was in getting the best out of a kitchen. The idea of having a role to play made her feel more confident and revived her spirits. She looked around the room for the tea urn. Never had the idea of a plain biscuit and a simple cup of tea seemed so desirable!

The footman who was presiding over the tea things poured her a cup of tea. It was blessedly hot, but it tasted of mushrooms, and the biscuits were stale and soft.

Alicia and Alicia's mother sat side-by-side on a circular window-seat. Good manners meant that Phoebe must smile at them and try to converse.

'What delicious tea,' she hazarded.

'I don't care for tea,' snapped Mrs Cooper. 'Smart people drink coffee.'

Alicia simply stared with nervous blue eyes.

Phoebe had often wondered what it would be like to wear a pretty dress and sit in a grand room and she had wished that she might try the experience. In reality, her head ached with the tension in the room. Much of it came from Miss Belmont who was a brooding bundle of self-pity. She was jealous, of course, and Phoebe could sympathise with her for whenever she thought of Felix and Alicia the green-eyed monster clawed at her own heart. The way he'd been so kind to her, more, the way he'd kissed her had lit a spark of hope in her breast and feelings in her heart, but, faced with the reality of the beautiful and wealthy Alicia Cooper, Phoebe knew that she'd have to crush any ideas of the magnificent Earl of Chando falling for his poor relation. It wasn't going to happen.

7

A few days later Felix was scowling over his morning letters. Sun slanted in through the long windows of the breakfast room, illuminating the dust. Robin lay full length on the sofa, counting days on his fingers.

'Shooting starts in thirteen days,' he announced.

No response came from Felix. Robin realised that his friend had been silent for what seemed a very long time, and that he hadn't touched his breakfast.

'What's the matter?'

'This letter is from Ravenscar. He wants to redeem the mortgage on Gosforth Farm.'

Robin sat bolt upright and ruffled his hair.

'What? What a pill! He can't do that. You've just drained all the marshes.'

'He can. It was very decent of him to

give me a mortgage in the first place.'

'What's made him change his mind?'

Felix shrugged.

'Reverses in his business, he says, whatever that may mean. I always suspected that he had dealings on the continent.'

'Well, if he lent money to the French he deserves all the reverses that are coming his way!' Robin exclaimed indignantly.

'It was stupid of me to start the drainage on a farm that wasn't mine, but geographically it was ideal for the experiment, and Ravenscar acted the gentleman when my father lost, that is, when the man acquired the property. I never thought of him repossessing.'

'Get another mortgage,' Robin suggested.

'There is no chance of my raising any money.'

Felix knew that a loan would be refused him, and word of that refusal might cause a panic and people would call in their bills.

'Never mind,' Robin said. 'It won't even leave a hole in your lands: Gosforth Farm is on the edge of the estate.'

'The very edge,' Felix said, with an attempt at a laugh, 'considering its location by the sea!'

His attempt at a laugh was not a success. The loss of family land hurt him. He felt unreasonably disappointed by the way Robin seemed to accept that the farm couldn't be saved. And now, here was that irritating Melville slipping into the room. Felix tried to ignore him, but the major domo hovered, waiting to be noticed.

'Yes?'

'Excuse me, my lord, but is it by your direction that SHE is in the kitchens this morning?'

'What?' Felix asked.

He didn't want to be bothered with domestic matters, yet Melville was buzzing away like a bluebottle on a window.

'It's only that if SHE were acting

upon your direction, I wouldn't care to deny her access to the pantries.'

Most of his mind was still struggling to comprehend the loss of his land and the waste of all the Dutch-inspired drainage improvements; the remaining tiny corner of his attention was busy with the implications of the Coopers' arrival. He didn't want to be bothered with domestic matters. He wished he could leap onto Kamil and gallop away to freedom. It seemed to him that the petty irritations of his new life were harder to bear than enemy fire, and Melville was still nagging.

'Adolphe is temperamental and if he were to be upset . . . '

Felix put down the horrible letter that had ruined his morning and turned to his duty.

'Who is this mysterious SHE and what are you complaining of?'

Melville rubbed his hands together.

'It's Miss Allen. She's inspecting the kitchens and upsetting the staff, if I may say so.'

'No you may not say so!' Felix bellowed. 'My cousin may go anywhere in this house that she wishes and you, and the other servants, are to follow her orders, and to pay her every respect. Is that clear?'

The major domo's jaw dropped.

'Very good, my lord.'

He bowed silently and oozed out of the room.

Robin stared at his friend in utter astonishment.

'Never heard you shout at an underling before!'

'It is long overdue in his case.'

'Know what you mean,' Robin observed sagely, drawing a fingertip through the dust on the sofa arm.

Felix couldn't help but smile at his friend.

'If even you have noticed the grime then things have reached a pretty pass.'

'Fellow's got a sneaky kind of look about him. I shouldn't like to trust him with the regimental supplies.'

'I have suspected for some time that

the rascal is fiddling with the accounts. Well, his cards are marked, but I've no time for him now. Mama will be expecting me.'

It took his mother about three seconds to see that he was not in his usual spirits.

'What is it, my dear?'

'Melville. It's a bore, but I shall have to take action.'

The dowager countess agreed.

'I have been thinking for some time that he is not the thing. The house gets ever dirtier. When I speak with him he smiles and agrees, but nothing is ever improved.'

'Good heavens, Mama! Why did you not tell me?'

'You have enough to worry about with the estate. What are a few cobwebs?'

Felix looked around him at his mother's cluttered room. Now that his eyes were open to the general neglect, he saw that all was dusty and uncared for.

'This room should have been cleaned when you were away at Eugenie's — a bottoming, do they call it?'

Georgiana dimpled at her son's interest in domestic affairs, and wondered what her father would have thought if he'd heard a real live earl discussing a bottoming. Her family had made a huge fortune from its factories, but in their anxiety to appear rather more aristocratic than they were, her parents had conditioned the girls to know nothing about the management of a house, and for a long time she hadn't needed to. However, she was realising, day by day, that she lacked the knowledge and weapons to combat Melville's increasing influence over the house.

'It is not of the least use asking me, my love,' she sighed. 'When dear old Barry was alive, the house ran like clockwork, but I haven't the slightest notion how he achieved it.'

Felix came to a decision.

'Peter, send word to Melville that I

wish to speak with him.'

The footman left, and in came Phoebe. She was singing, and Pepe trotted obediently at her heels.

'Is that one of Mr Mozart's lovely songs?' asked the dowager countess, smiling.

Phoebe started guiltily.

'Yes. I hope you don't mind. It is a habit of mine to sing while I'm working.'

Felix stirred, his raking glance taking in the orphanage gown and white pinafore.

'What, pray, might my mother's guest be working at?'

'I can tell you that!' bleated a high, thin voice.

Miss Belmont trotted into the room, her gooseberry eyes gleaming in excitement under her sparse lashes. 'She's been meddling in the kitchen! To inspect one's host's kitchen! I never heard of such rudeness in my life!'

Phoebe's hand flew to her mouth.

'I had no thought of being rude!'

She felt guilty as she became aware that Felix was looking at her in a straight-faced, assessing manner. She was not physically pinned to the spot by his raking green gaze, of course, but if she were to turn away from him, she felt that she might appear skittish, and she wanted to appear calm.

She'd done her best to argue away her feelings for the man. Looking back she realised that not a word had been said between them. It had all been unspoken, a matter of feelings, and possibly of feelings on her side alone. Yes, he had kissed her, and that was very wrong of him, but what if it had meant nothing to him? It was a moment caused by moonlight and magic and the hot punch at the fair. What if only she felt the magic?

Phoebe, who had been accustomed to fall into her shared attic couch and sleep like the dead for every hour she was able, had tossed and turned in her comfortable tester bed all the previous night. Staring up at the embroidered hangings she reminded herself that one thing was for sure: she had enough pride to not let him know how he made her feel.

She reminded herself of this decision now, ignored the shivering vibrations in her stomach, and her sinking feeling of being in the wrong, and she returned his gaze as directly as she could.

'I simply wished to be useful,' she fudged.

'Phoebe,' Felix asked, in tones of gentle wonder. 'How exactly could my cousin be useful in the kitchens?'

There was no withstanding him; she would have to confess.

'I have been checking up on the chef.'

Miss Belmont fairly twitched with the force of her feelings.

'You dare to admit it? You dare to find fault with the housekeeping at Elwood? You are the worst-mannered girl I ever encountered.'

'Miss Belmont!' Felix warned.

'Cousin Thalia,' Georgiana protested.

But there was no stopping her.

'How do you think Lady Chando feels about your abominable cheek? How dare you behave in such an unladylike manner? If I had my way you'd be packing your bags this very minute.'

'MISS BELMONT!' thundered Felix.

Phoebe spoke nervously into the silence that followed.

'I assumed that you asked me here to be useful.'

Georgiana smiled gently.

'I wished only for your company.'

'I'm sorry if I have done wrong, but work is a habit with me, and there seemed much to be done.'

Miss Belmont twitched violently, but Felix glared at her and she subsided.

'Miss Allen,' he asked a second time, because he truly wanted to know, 'what could you possibly find to take care of in the kitchens of Elwood?'

'Adolphe is suffering from complete nervous exhaustion! I suspected that it might be so from the disgraceful dinner last night.'

Felix and his mother stared ahead for one stunned second, and then they turned to look at one another, green gazes locking. Not registering their slowly-dawning smiles, Phoebe put a hand to her mouth.

'Oh! I am so sorry! I am being critical again. Only, pray forgive me, but he is serving you food that is making you ill.'

Georgiana's smile turned rueful.

'Well, I own that I was awake for some time last night wrestling with the fish tails.'

'I'm sure the situation could be remedied,' Phoebe ventured. 'If you would just allow me . . . '

And suddenly the dowager countess breathed a huge sigh and turned her soft green gaze on to Phoebe.

'My dear, if you could manage Adolphe's nerves I would be eternally grateful.'

'I think I already know how to handle Adolphe.'

Felix said sharply, 'Why should you

be troubled with the housekeeping?'

'Why should your mother be burdened when she is not well?'

Felix's expression was baffled.

'But you are a guest.'

'And never was a guest so happy and comfortable! I adore my yellow room.'

Georgiana looked astonished.

'I gave orders that you be put in the rose suite, and that is pink. We keep the little yellow room for visiting children and their governesses. Ah, here is Melville now. He will be able to explain, I'm sure.'

The major domo entered the room warily, like a wild animal scenting a trap. His dark, beadlike eyes darted around the room. He bowed low.

'A mouse was found in the rose suite, my lady, and so I placed the young lady in the yellow room as a temporary measure.'

He cast a satisfied glance at the dowager countess, obviously feeling that he'd wriggled out of trouble, but Felix was unyielding.

'You are failing sadly in your duties if vermin are to be found in the house. I think your position may need rethinking,' he continued gently. 'You seem to be neglecting your duties.'

The shining beads of Melville's eyes flashed.

'But I manage the servants and I look after the silver and I protect the house — '

'I am beginning to wonder if it is not the house that needs protecting from your depredations.'

Melville's expression was that of a petty dictator who has been deposed.

'You can't prove anything!'

'You may prefer to leave before I look for proof because I will call the magistrate if I find any. See John Adam about your wages, of course.'

'Wages!' Melville yelled. 'That's not — '

He stopped himself, but Felix finished for him.

'That's not the main perk of this position?'

Melville spat on the floor.

A shocked silence ensued. Then the major domo turned and flounced out, slamming the door behind him. Felix spoke to the footman.

'Peter, follow Melville out, if you please. I'd like him to be accompanied until he has packed and left the estate.'

The footman grinned hugely and went out. Felix turned to his mother's companion.

'Miss Belmont, if you would be so good as to send for Sam. He will clear up this mess.'

'I'm far too upset,' she bleated. She drew out a silver bottle of smelling salts. 'Chando, my nerves! I am quite overcome! It's not what I've been used to! My heart! It's fluttering!'

You didn't need to feel the woman's pulse to know that she was thoroughly enjoying the drama.

Felix glared at Miss Belmont, and opened his mouth, but then he cast a glance at Phoebe and visibly controlled himself. A glance of perfect understanding passed between them and she knew he was remembering her lecture on the horrors of being a poor dependent.

'I'll go,' Phoebe offered, laughing, and she let her smile tell him that she appreciated his restraint.

She fetched Jenny first, who took one look at Georgiana and ran for brandy. The dresser made her mistress sip the amber liquid, and then stood watching the colour come back into the dowager countess's cheeks. She smiled approvingly.

'You'll be recovered in a second or two. It'll be better for us all now that nasty tyrant has gone!'

The dowager countess was recovering from her shock. She looked up with an alert expression.

'Jenny, why did you not mention that Phoebe was pushed away in the yellow room?'

'Melville said it was your orders.'

Georgiana said contritely, 'It's my fault for not being able to run a house. If Miss Allen is truly willing to supervise the housekeeping, it will be a blessing.'

Miss Belmont let out a great bleat.

'What? You are to let that nobody give orders? I do my poor best and this is all the thanks I get! To have my authority usurped! I work my fingers to the bone . . . '

Jenny bustled over to the hysterical companion and put a hand under her arm.

'You need a nice rest on your bed,' she said sharply.

Miss Belmont had enough sense left to allow herself to be helped out of the room. Felix and his mother shared another glance. She looked into his face with her usual penetration.

'What a silly and unpleasant scene. Domestic troubles should be no concern of yours and I wish I could have spared you. Yet I fear there is more amiss with you than this troublesome house.'

Maybe a mother's magic could find a way out of his horrible predicament.

'I am to lose Gosforth Farm,' he admitted, explaining. 'It is a reverse, as you have perceived.'

'How provoking!'

'It could have been any one of a dozen properties, considering the mortgages we carry,' Felix said, bitterly. 'Our position is so precarious. I will not be easy until we are out of debt.'

She looked tenderly into his face, her green eyes loving.

'You have done so well, dearest. Forget Gosforth Farm. It is nothing, but nothing, compared to what you have saved.'

It had been foolish of him to expect his mother to help. No one could mend the pain he felt.

The door opened and Phoebe came in with Pepe at her heels. She was followed by Sam, two footmen and a scullery boy carrying a bucket of water.

Felix looked at the head footman.

'Please have Miss Allen moved into the rose suite.'

Sam's broad smile lit his eyes.

'With your permission, it might be better if Miss Allen were to stay where she is for a day or so, while we fettle it.'

Felix felt ashamed that the house was in such disarray, and furious that a whole morning was ticking away, wasted on domestic trivia. He made himself speak softly to the footman.

'Sam, you are in charge.'

Phoebe gave a merry smile.

'We shall go on much better with Sam at the helm. But Felix, may I suggest — '

'You may not!' he snapped.

He saw the hurt bloom in her grey eyes. He felt like a brute.

'My dear cousin, I simply meant that there is no need to ask me first. You must treat the house as your own. Do as you please!'

Her dimples showed tentatively.

'I was only going to suggest that we make your mama comfortable first. I cannot understand why her room was not thoroughly cleaned while she was away at her sister Eugenie's.'

On hearing his own thoughts echoed so neatly, Felix threw up his hands.

'Sam, you are to take your orders from Miss Allen.'

'I'll do that with pleasure, my lord. She'll make it come good, you'll see.'

Felix noticed that Sam, Jenny, the footmen and the scullery boy were all beaming. It looked as if Phoebe had completely won over the servants. He didn't know whether irritation or respect was his uppermost feeling, and in any case, he had a thousand more urgent things to deal with this day.

'Do you need me?'

The head footman's honest smile lit up his face.

'You leave it to me and Miss Allen, my lord.'

And Felix was glad to do so.

Caldicott was waiting patiently for him in the morning room. He was a thoroughly reliable old-fashioned lawyer with steady brown eyes.

'I'm sorry to have kept you waiting,' Felix said, 'and I'm even sorrier to inform you that Gosforth Farm is lost to us.'

As he explained, he realised that he had been hoping that Caldicott would have a miracle solution to offer, but the lawyer, although shocked, accepted that the case was hopeless. He shook his white wig gloomily.

'There is no possible way to raise any money. The land will indeed have to go back to Ravenscar.'

They worked on until lunchtime, when they emerged from the morning room to hear a female voice singing blithely in the hall.

Felix felt a smile tug at his lips, dispelling his gloom, just a little.

'I do not think that you have met the lost relative that you so skilfully located for us.'

He watched Caldicott's face carefully while he performed the introductions between his formally correct lawyer and Phoebe, who was still wearing not only her orphanage gown, but also her white apron as well. The lawyer's face remained admirably straight, but there was shocked outrage in the depths of his brown eyes! His bow was several stages stiffer than usual as he departed, pausing for only long enough to say again what a great shame it was to lose Gosforth Farm.

As soon as the door closed behind him Felix turned to Phoebe.

'My dear cousin, pray forgive me, but, your attire . . . '

She regarded him with those brilliant grey eyes.

'Ah! So that was his problem. But am I to care what a lawyer, even such a terrifyingly stiff and old-fashioned lawyer such as Caldicott, thinks of me?'

Put in those terms, it was not difficult to answer.

'Well, no, and you must do as you wish. But Miss Allen, there is not the least need for you to concern yourself with household matters.'

Phoebe's brisk glance swept the cluttered, muddled and generally disgraceful hall. She thought that the clear light of day showed that there was a pressing need for her to get involved with the house, but she had not missed the way that Felix kept stealing little looks at her hair, which was back in its plain, everyday arrangement, and her apron. She was pretty certain that he disapproved. He made her feel exposed and out of place again, so she steadied her chin and spoke with as much self-assurance as she could muster.

'Would you have me sit on a sofa and flip through the ladies' journals and leave everything to worry your poor mama?'

He smiled, a half-smile, that's all it was, a slight quirk of the lips that held surprise at her defiance. Phoebe felt her breath quicken and realised all over again how dangerous his charm was.

'You are very adroit, cousin! You pick on the one argument that I cannot withstand. My mama's comfort is paramount. But Miss Allen, please believe me, you were not invited here to be made use of as a domestic drudge, or to be a downtrodden companion.'

His green eyes were bright with memories. How dangerous was the sense of shared understanding that flowed between them.

'Shall we go in for luncheon?' Felix asked.

Of course the room was cluttered, dirty and fusty. Luncheon, which was already laid out on the sideboards, seemed to consist mainly of rich, greasy pastries and cakes oozing not very fresh cream. Phoebe judged it better to ignore the quality of the food, for now, and to turn the conversation to non-domestic matters. She smiled and tried to speak jokingly.

'Will it make you happy to know that the dressmaker is coming this afternoon? I own that a new gown will be very pleasant.'

Felix's lazy half smile came again, along with an, 'Indeed, I'm very glad to hear it,' but the smile faded, and Phoebe could tell that his thoughts had left her, and not gone, it seemed to her, into pleasant channels.

'Did I hear Caldicott say that Gosforth Farm was to be sold? Surely that is the land that you had drained at so much trouble and expense?'

'You are frighteningly efficient, Miss Allen. It is marvellous how quickly you have become familiar with Elwood.'

Felix's face was a polite social mask, but Phoebe could read his green eyes better than he knew. His smile did not fool her. The loss was hurting him dreadfully. It seemed natural to coax him.

'Tell me!' Phoebe commanded.

Twenty minutes later Felix was saying with wonder in his green eyes, 'How strange! I have told you more than anyone. I will of course, appear stoic about my loss with others.'

'Or not lose the farm at all,' Phoebe suggested.

His gaze locked on her face, stunning her with its impact.

'Have you not listened? I have no way of meeting that mortgage.'

Phoebe had to push her chair back, to make a little space between them to escape from his force, but she wasn't cowed.

'There's always a way.'

'My lawyer and my man of business say it's impossible.'

'I am sure you can raise the cash!'

'Tell me how and I shall be glad to do so!'

A tense, uneasy silence fell.

Phoebe, forgetting that there were footmen in the room who were waiting to serve her, got up and walked to the sideboard, hoping to find a piece of fruit or something edible. She also needed some distance from his physical presence. She thought she had escaped from him, but just as she was taking a deep shaky breath, Felix's voice came from barely an inch behind her.

'Content yourself with reorganising the house from attic to cellar and leave business matters to men who understand them.'

She whipped around. Yes, he was

standing less than an inch away from her, but something in his words had triggered an idea.

'From attic to cellar,' she repeated thoughtfully. 'There is a vast quantity of French wine in your cellars. Where did such tremendous quantities of wine come from?'

'My Uncle Edmund married a French countess from Burgundy. When he saw the troubles coming, he shipped a prodigious amount of wine to Elwood for safe keeping.'

'Is the wine valuable?'

Felix raised his eyebrows and gave her a deeply masculine look.

'The price of household goods is hardly my province.'

'It is now!' she informed him briskly.

He'd closed the gap between them again. Needing to break away from the feeling of being too close to his body, she returned to the table. He followed. She could feel his presence by the fine hairs on her body. She had so many feelings to hide from him, but she knew that her grand idea would distract him.

'Why do you not sell the wine?'

'Do you take me for a merchant?'

'You have wine to sell and need of money.'

'You would have me enter trade?'

'Why not?'

Felix's green eyes held an interesting mix of disdain, male superiority and downright pig-headedness as he declared, 'It's simply not the done thing.'

Phoebe hesitated, wanting to persuade him, but knowing that by hinting at his father's draining of the estate's assets she was on dangerous ground.

'You do know that it is possible to sell objects from the estate when money is needed.'

Yes, that touched a nerve. His mood turned icy.

'My duty is to restore this estate! I will not allow it to be exploited and pillaged.'

'I am not suggesting that you touch valuable assets; only that you dispose of unnecessary luxury items.'

'I am not a tradesman.'

Phoebe wanted to shake his shoulders and tell him not to be such a snob, but she stuck to cool reason and tried not to let her tone sound exasperated.

'Think of saving your land, not losing your dignity! If there is no auction house in Lancaster the wine can be sold in London. You need not be personally involved.'

Felix gave her a long, intent look. His green eyes were angry and probing. She'd stirred him up and he was intent on revenge.

'How do you know about such vulgar business practices?'

It was hard to face him. His gaze penetrated the protective skin she'd grown following her father's death. She gasped, the pain raw again for an instant, but if she were to persuade him, she would have to tell him her story.

'There was nothing when Papa died, nothing but debts. I had to arrange to sell his wine, his books, the pastel portrait Thomas Laurence did of my mother. Believe me, how to raise money from the sale of household goods was knowledge hard come by.'

His features gave nothing away as he silently studied her. She held her breath and waited.

'I see,' he said slowly.

I see? I see? Was that all he had to say to her after she'd just bared her soul to him? Phoebe rose to her feet in a daze. He did not call after her. She walked as steadily as she could out of the room and across the cluttered hall. She hardly noticed the footmen opening the doors or little Pepe scampering to follow her. She was in a blind rage as she mounted the sweep of the staircase. I see? Did he not realise that she was doing her best to help him? If he was so proud and so stupid and so stubborn that he'd rather have a few bottles of plonk than a decent working farm then she was through with him. She wasn't going to stay in a place where she wasn't appreciated!

Gaining the safety of the yellow room, Phoebe relieved her feelings by giving the door a hearty slam. She paced the floor angrily. I see? The only likeness of her mother gone for ever and all he can say is, I see? Did he think she was made of stone? That it had been easy for her to talk about selling her old life? That anything to do with him was easy for her, feeling about him the way she did?

Her legs folded and she sank to the floor, pulled her knees to her chest, buried her face in them and sobbed bitterly. Pepe nuzzled at her in sympathy, licking the hot tears that flowed down her face.

Her tears soon faded, she wasn't much given to crying. And she knew, too, the real reason for her tears. She saw nothing but trouble ahead, and she had only herself to blame.

8

Felix wanted to follow Phoebe, but Mr Cooper chose that moment to enter the room. The earl had never been less pleased to see a magenta waistcoat advancing towards him. He was even more displeased by the businessman's opening remarks.

'Too bad the farm you are having to sell is the very one you spent so much money on.'

'I won't be selling it,' Felix flared.

The raised eyebrow that greeted his defiance reminded him that Mr Cooper knew everything about his perilous financial state.

'Oh, aye, got a plan have you?'

And Felix found that he had. He didn't know quite how Phoebe had won him over to her way of thinking, that was a puzzle he'd consider later, but her idea was sound. He was no longer falling into a pit of loss and despair. His feelings had changed. He wasn't going to lose Gosforth Farm. Why should he not sell his wine? He knew that he might attract gossip, but he didn't care. Phoebe had the right of it. A flash of warmth twined around his heart as her image flashed into his brain. If it hadn't been for her, he would have lost his good land. He smiled at the tradesman.

'There is a quantity of good French wine in the cellars. I shall dispose of it and settle the mortgage with the proceeds.'

'That is a workable plan,' approved Mr Cooper. 'I know a wine merchant in Bath who'd be glad to help you out. He caters for the Prince Regent so he's always on the look out for luxury wines. He's a big pal of mine. Do you want me to contact him?'

Felix accepted with gratitude, and the two men quickly settled the details. Mr Cooper looked up from his notes with regret in his blue eyes.

'Are you sure you couldn't fancy my

daughter, Chando? I'll admit I only came here to buy her a title, but I like the cut of your jib, and this estate's a beauty, or at least, if I drop a bit of blunt on it, it could be.'

'Why would you want your daughter to marry Elwood?'

'Why shouldn't she be happy here?'

'Because Elwood demands your life, your freedom, your independence forever,' Felix said with feeling. 'You think about it night and day; you worry about it; work for it; spend your last gasp in its service. Are you sure that's what you want for your daughter?'

'Maybe not, when you put it like that, but my wife is a very determined woman, and she's determined on a title and a grand house for my girl.'

'Have you told her that she will have to look for a husband elsewhere?'

The tradesman coughed.

'I didn't like to disappoint her, nor betray your confidences. She'll realise the truth soon enough. Now, when can you give me a list of this wine?'

'I'll see to it right away.'

Felix didn't know whether to be amused or annoyed when he heard that Phoebe was already busy in the wine cellars. He got one of the footmen to light a candelabrum and show him where she was working.

Phoebe turned her dark head when she saw him coming. She lifted her lantern so that the glow illuminated her face. The wary sadness in her eyes stirred uncomfortable emotions within him.

'I wanted to find some nice wine for dinner tonight,' she said defensively.

Felix held out a hand to her.

'Cousin, can you forgive me? I was slow on the uptake this morning, but once again it seems, I have come around to your way of thinking. I am going to sell the wine.'

Phoebe was barely able to suppress a tiny moan of relief. The most dreadful feeling of guilt had washed over her when she saw his tall figure approaching, and she realised that she'd been afraid that he was going to tell her off. Now she felt a heavenly smile spreading over her features. It was so good of him to come himself.

He smiled back, and, suddenly, shockingly in the cool damp air of the cellars, that heat flashed between them again. It radiated from him in warm pulses. Did he feel the same heat from her? Phoebe wondered. It would be so easy to step forward and let her soft female figure flow against his lean, hard body, to soak in the clean scent of soap that emanated from him.

She hoped and prayed that Felix would never know what she was thinking! She needed to cut herself off from the physical plane and return to everyday matters at once.

Felix stepped away from her as if he'd come to the same decision. He told the footman to place the candelabrum so that it illuminated the vaulted stone arches and then he told him to make a list of all the wine in the cellar.

'These are the old dungeons,' he

observed to Phoebe, his voice a deep rumble. 'The stone didn't burn when the castle fell.'

With an effort, Phoebe snatched in a breath and maintained her outward composure. She swept an arm around the cobwebby vastness.

'It's very scenic, is it not? Quite Gothic, and remarkably full of wine.'

Felix turned his head to survey the ranks of barrels. There must have been at least thirty casks in this cavern alone. He knocked on the nearest wooden barrel, huge in its metal rack.

'This one is still full by the sound of it.'

'They all are, and come this way,' Phoebe said, leading him deeper into the cellars. 'There is a vast quantity of brandy in this alcove.'

They explored for a few minutes longer, but Phoebe sensed that Felix had made his decision and found out the facts, and now he was ready to move on to other matters.

Felix and Phoebe left the kitchens

and walked into the hall. The grand hall seemed to be the heart of the house, Phoebe reflected. You naturally seemed to end up there. What a pity it was so filthy and cluttered.

'Are all these portraits of family members?' she enquired, looking at the confusion of paintings that smothered the walls.

Something was making Felix feel tetchy.

'Do you want me to sell my ancestors?'

'Oh no!' Phoebe cried. She gestured to one particular picture by Hogarth. 'But I wonder that anyone should care to have this drunken party on their wall.'

Felix meant to tell her coldly that her criticism of his father's taste was inappropriate, but then he saw that she was watching his displeasure with a small crinkle of bewilderment in her forehead. She looked so small and vulnerable that his anger died.

'What do you think?' she urged him.

Felix felt a jolt in his heart as he examined the depiction of unbridled excess on the wall before him. As a reminder of his papa's many failings and extravagances she could hardly have picked a painting he less wished to keep.

'My father was fond of Hogarth,' he replied. 'But I agree that not all of his work is suitable for public display.'

'Here's another of his pictures!' Phoebe cried, and then her cheeks went a delicious pink. 'I think, Felix, that I had better not look at it too closely.'

Felix should never have looked at a picture that depicted lovemaking, given his attraction to Phoebe. It put dangerous ideas in his head. She was standing close to him, and he could smell roses.

In the eyes of the world they were merely two cousins, standing in the open hall, discussing his father's art collection. In his mind he was imagining a kiss that had nothing gentle about it.

He felt a fierce hunger that wouldn't be contained. He wanted to press his lips into Phoebe's and turn her to his will. A fever rose in him and burned, craving an outlet. He wanted to twist his hands into her hair, anchoring her to hold her close, and he wanted her mouth to reply to him violently. He ached to feel her lips move beneath him, and yet for all the wildness of his desire, he had never felt so tenderly towards a woman in his life.

He hoped and prayed she would never guess what he'd been thinking. He pressed a hand to his forehead and drew in a ragged breath. He was furious with himself for losing control. It would not happen again. It annoyed him that he reacted to Phoebe in this passionate way. He'd never had such wild feelings before.

'I'll have those pictures burned.'

'My lord, you must not destroy them!' Phoebe cried. Her grey eyes shone very bright. 'Do you not know that one of Hogarth's paintings was sold for a thousand guineas last year?'

A sudden fierce hope opened doors in Felix's mind.

'One thousand guineas?' he repeated slowly.

And the thought of his loans and his mortgages and the hateful business of being beholden to money lenders crawled though his mind, but now there was a vision of freedom to oppose his burdens. Dare he take this way out? Was he man enough to brave what society would say if he were to sell off his father's art collection?

He looked at Phoebe and there were clearly no doubts in her mind. She had moved on to practical matters.

'Has anyone catalogued Elwood's paintings and artefacts?' Phoebe asked.

'Never,' he answered, somehow not minding that she knew the truth. In fact it was a blessed relief to be able to say frankly, 'Surely by now you have realised that the house is in complete disarray?'

'All this artwork should be listed and

sorted. Then you can decide what to keep and what to dispose of.'

Felix watched her curiously. He'd never met such a confident and capable woman, but he liked it. He liked the way her grey eyes narrowed when she thought. He liked the grave little air with which she made her pronouncements. He knew that his agent or his lawyer could advise him, but an imp in him wanted to test her abilities further.

'Where should we send the items that are to be sold?'

'There is a company called Christie's in Pall Mall. They were very good to me. They knew how hard it was for me to part with Mama's portrait.'

'Did your papa commission the picture from Lawrence?'

'No. They were friends because Papa was at college with his brother. Lawrence made the picture for fun. It was just before Mama died.'

Felix wanted to take away the sad look in her eyes. At that moment he resolved to track down the picture and return it to her.

'What news?' rang out a cheerful voice as Robin joined them.

For a moment Felix wanted to throttle his old friend, and then he took a cool breath and realised that he had been saved from exposing himself to Phoebe. Where had that impulse to buy her a gift come from? Once again he was astonished by how strongly he felt about her. He didn't want to be ridden by feelings and impulses. He didn't want emotion to tear into the walls that he'd built around his world and unsettle him. He wanted nothing to endanger his hard-won control. He had to struggle to hide the turmoil that he was feeling inside, and that annoyed him. It was an effort to smile at Robin.

'We have much to tell you! Would you be very surprised if I told you that I am to become a merchant?'

Robin's eyes opened very wide at first, but after only a few moments of reflection, he was enthusiastic.

'You must have quantities of stuff

that no-one would miss. Do you remember that wet day when we decided to practise fencing in the attics? The rooms were stuffed so full of sooty boxes and bundles that we couldn't make space, so we went ratting in the stables instead.'

'Sooty boxes?' Phoebe asked, an interested light glowing in her grey eyes.

'It'll be what was saved from the fire when the castle burned down,' Felix said. 'I suppose it was put away for so long it was forgotten about. And my grandfather didn't want anything old. He was in love with the classical style, as you can see from the house.'

'It's a beautiful house,' Phoebe said. 'But I do wonder why the new house wasn't built up on the hill with those glorious open views across the coast.'

'Pirates!' Felix told her.

Her astonished face amused him.

'My ancestors were canny. There was always the hope that raiders would sail straight past, if the house could not be seen from the sea.'

Phoebe's dark lashes swept down and then up in a blink of surprise and Felix laughed at her.

'It is not so very long ago that the American pirate, Paul Jones, sacked Whitehaven and a nearby castle.'

But she was not to be teased.

'Did you not know that his father had worked in the gardens for the Earl of Selkirk? One suspects a grudge of some kind.'

Robin chuckled.

'One should never debate with a schoolmarm. They have such quantities of facts at their fingertips to argue with. Come, Miss Allen. I bet you can inform us what antiquities are popular this season.'

'Not exactly,' she replied, smiling into his blue eyes in a way that made Felix want to give his old friend a jealous punch on the jaw. 'But we may be in luck, for Gothic is much the rage. I must find out what treasures we have.'

Felix stared into Phoebe's eyes. They

sparkled and glowed. Grey is considered a cool colour, but Phoebe's eyes were warm and merry. He would never forget that moment of contact as long as he lived. Phoebe's picture was caught safe in his heart for ever. The severe arrangement of her hair and the plainness of her gown had the effect of emphasising the blazing radiant vitality of the woman before him. His surroundings seemed to fade away, along with the sound of Robin chatting about selling suits of armour to city bankers. It was as if they were alone with each other, and his desire was a fire in his circulating blood. He had never felt such desire for a woman before. It unsettled him that desire had returned to taunt him. It wasn't who he was. He'd never wanted to feel the passion that made such fools of men, and he wasn't going to allow himself to begin feeling it now. One passion could lead to another, and there was no way he would allow himself to be taken over by the desire to drink, to gamble, to seek out pleasure at the expense of one's good name. No feelings were going to make a fool out of him.

'The dressmaker is here for Miss Allen,' a voice was saying behind them.

Phoebe turned to smile at the footman.

'I shall be with you in a minute.'

Then she turned to Felix.

'My lord, unless you should dislike it immensely, I should like to investigate those attics.' Sudden dimples showed, making her face so pretty. 'I couldn't leave such a delicious task to anyone else.' She looked into his eyes, searching them, and he was aware of a strong current of sympathy. 'That is, unless you wish the items to be left undisturbed?'

Felix had himself back in check.

'You must do as you please, cousin.'

He even found a smile.

'I am using that phrase very frequently, am I not? But indeed, I do wish to proceed with the project.'

Her lovely grey eyes met his for a

second longer, and then she curtseyed, and then whisked up the stairs with Pepe scampering after her.

Felix watched her go, shocked to see what could only be shabby orphanage slippers twinkling under the skirts of the grey gown. He was immune to the slenderness of her figure and the grace of her carriage. His earlier blaze of passion was safely under control, but different feelings about Phoebe now filled his heart, and these feelings although unfamiliar, were not wholly unwelcome to him. He was flooded with a sensation of wellbeing. He felt totally, deeply comforted. Who else but Phoebe could have produced a way to turn the irritating muddle and clutter of Elwood into good productive land? She was Dutch engineering for the soul.

He imagined herds of fat sheep grazing on his marshes, his marshes, to be protected and watched over and passed on forever. His heart lifted with a pure, uncomplicated exultation that he had not felt since before the black day he'd had to tell his colonel that his father was dead and that he was leaving his beloved regiment.

Phoebe's trim form vanished into the gallery. Unconsciously, he let out a deep breath. Robin turned to him smiling.

'Miss Allen may not be in the regular style, but by Jove, I don't know when I met a more attractive female. She's quality through and through. She's dashed pretty, too.'

Primitive possessiveness rose up in Felix, and it must have shown in his expression. Robin was so alarmed that his hand automatically moved to where his sword hilt should be.

'Message received, old chap! I'm not to romance your cousin.'

'You talk a great deal of nonsense, Robin, but you have your uses. Do you care to accompany me while I break the news to Mama that we are to join the merchant class? I may escape with my life if you are there to protect me.'

9

Phoebe pushed open the door to her yellow room. The scene was as busy as an Indian bazaar. Her room was full of people spreading out lengths of printed muslin. The bolts of brightly-coloured fabric fluttered in a giddy riot of colour. Female voices rose to the ceiling in happy chatter. Pepe gave a little whine and put his tail between his legs.

Kitty raced to meet her.

'Oh, Miss Phoebe! Come and look! You never saw such beautiful material!'

Phoebe could now see several strangers looking at her, the dressmaker and her assistants. They had sent five people to wait on her? Oh my gosh! How much money would they expect her to spend?

'I hope you will not be disappointed with the smallness of my order,' she murmured.

A middle-aged lady in a pretty, but respectable, striped gown moved forward and curtseyed.

'I quite understand that you will be ordering most of your wardrobe in London.' The woman had a nice open face, and she gave a confident smile. 'However, I think you'll be pleased, and maybe surprised, when you see what my workshops can produce for you.'

Jenny bustled forward, her brown eyes merry.

'The dowager countess says you are to be sure to bespeak a riding habit as well as a walking dress, something for the evening, some pretty muslins and a ball gown.'

Miss Michaels whipped out a tape measure and bent down to take Phoebe's measurements, clicking her tongue regretfully over the lack of height, but praising her dainty proportions. Phoebe stared at Jenny over the dressmaker's head, knowing that her cheeks were crimson.

'Jenny,' she said awkwardly, 'you are

surely aware that I must practise economy.'

Jenny's smile split her face.

'Bless, you, Miss Allen, you leave that to the dowager countess. She has issued a list of clothes that she wishes you to have, just to tide you over. They are her gift to you.'

Miss Michaels lifted her face to agree.

'It's all taken care of, my dear.'

The array of patterns, fabrics and trimmings on offer made Phoebe practically weep with ecstasy. Only a woman who had worn nothing but grey gowns and white aprons for three years could have fully understood the joy that the yards of sprigged muslin, striped wool and shimmering silk aroused in her heart. She spent three blissful hours sorting through the piles, holding fabrics next to her face in front of the looking glass, having lengths of beautiful colours draped and pinned around her, changing her mind as to which pattern suited which fabric, going back to her first choice, and never once feeling that anyone was cross or impatient with her. It was heaven!

The dressmaker had brought several shells of garments with her, and once she had the measurements and Phoebe had made her choices, the assistants were set to altering one of the half-made garments to her measurements.

'You must have something pretty to wear tonight,' Miss Michaels said, smiling.

The violet dress suited Phoebe like a dream. The colour was vivid without being bright, and made her grey eyes seem to blaze out of her face. The high waistline and puff sleeves flattered her figure, and the half train added elegance.

'I almost look tall, don't I?' Phoebe said, examining her reflection in the looking glass.

She felt pretty, transformed, and she couldn't help wondering if Felix would notice, and approve.

The walk downstairs had lost its terrors now she knew where to go. She swished confidently past the walls of portraits and swept down the grand staircase. Her good feelings lasted until she joined the group in the hall by the huge marble fireplace and saw Alicia Cooper standing in front of the blazing fire.

Alicia wore a gown that was a perfect concoction of crimson and pale orange silk. She was too shy to look at Phoebe, but her mother lifted her head and looked straight at Phoebe with forceful blue eyes. It was a direct, challenging gaze, almost angry. A scornful smile touched her red mouth, and then she turned away, and Phoebe immediately felt of no account.

Anyone would resent that disdainful look, she thought. With a sinking heart she reminded herself that she was the poor relative, and Alicia was to be mistress of the house. Everything is wrong, thought Phoebe dismally, and despite giving herself a good talking-to on the subject of fortunes and how lucky she was to have one, she remained subdued all through the evening.

But maybe the talking-to did have an effect. Her spirits had returned to almost normal by the next morning. She sat up in her delightful tester bed and looked out of the long windows. It was a fine, blustery day, with fat white clouds racing over the sky. Pepe was in his basket by the fire, but he lifted his little head and wagged his tail when he saw her looking at him.

She could hear noise and bustle in the bathroom, and Jenny popped her head out of the door. She came into the yellow room and dropped a curtsey when she saw Phoebe was awake.

'Good morning, Miss Allen. Kitty is running you a bath. What will you wear this morning?'

'I'll wear my grey gown and white apron, if you please.'

It was the wrong answer. Jenny's demeanour was prim, but her words were determined.

'Your old garments have been disposed of, Miss Allen.'

'What a waste,' Phoebe said, feeling thwarted, and slightly suspicious. 'You'll have to get them back. What am I to wear to go up into the attics?'

'Miss Allen, may I speak frankly?'

Phoebe looked at the woman's open face and steady hazel eyes and felt nothing but goodwill emanating from her.

'What is it?'

'It is not at all the thing for the dowager countess's guest to run around in a shabby pinafore. If you do not mind for yourself, do please think of her feelings.'

Phoebe felt stabbed to the heart.

'I am so used to getting up, putting on a pinafore and setting to work, that it didn't occur to me that it truly wasn't proper.'

'Things change, Miss Allen.'

Phoebe's brow puckered as she thought over the situation.

'I'm still going up to the attics!' she

pronounced. 'They will hardly come to me!'

'Oh, but they will,' Jenny said gently. 'Why do you not order the servants to empty the attics?'

'Ah!' Phoebe said, as a light dawned. 'I could have them wash and clean each piece before the items are described and catalogued. I must find an empty room where we can work.'

The proper face creased into a smile that crinkled the abigail's features into a warm expression.

'The dressmaker delivered a very smart, dark-green morning gown that is suitable for working in. Would you care to try it on?'

Phoebe was too good a manager of people herself not to recognise the woman's tactics, but it was curiously restful to be told how to go on, and in all honesty what did she know about life in a grand house? It was a comfort to know that Jenny was looking out for her and would help her to behave correctly.

For the next few days, whenever she looked at her reflection in the looking glass, she was overcome with a sense of unreality. The green dress was simple, and elegant, plainly expensive and like nothing she'd ever worn before. Jenny arranged her hair into sophisticated curls every morning, and one night she did mysterious things with threads and scissors that tamed Phoebe's eyebrows into aristocratic curves.

Kitty, who was Jenny's faithful handmaiden and biggest admirer, watched every move, vowing to learn how it was done. She loved her new lavender frocks and was openly revelling in every moment of their new life. Phoebe noticed that she hardly seemed interested in the news when a letter arrived from Miss Pennyfeather. In turn, the letter made it clear that life at the seminary was settling down without Phoebe and Kitty and they were in a fair way to being forgotten themselves, which was just as it should be.

'Life flows on like a river,' Phoebe sang as she went downstairs one evening.

The grand surroundings didn't intimidate her half so much now she had new clothes!

A new person had joined the group in the hall, a young man with flowing locks and an air of theatricality.

'Gordon Gordon-Rose is on the way to the Lake District to stay with some friends and write poetry,' the curate explained, as he performed the introductions. 'Of course the poetry is just a hobby: on vacation from Cambridge, aren't you, Gordon-Rose? Theology and the classics, isn't it?'

The poet nodded dreamily. Miss Belmont piped up.

'He always visits Elwood to see me. I'm his favourite aunt.'

It was the first time that Miss Belmont had spoken voluntarily to Phoebe. Thalia's cheeks were pink with excitement. The young man didn't seem so thrilled with his aunt's company, and so it was no surprise when he confided at dinner that he was hoping to touch his aunt for a handout.

'Cambridge is so expensive,' he complained.

The poet had gooseberry-green eyes just like his aunt's, and a weak mouth, Phoebe noticed.

'Wouldn't a post of some kind give you more independence?' she suggested.

He puffed out his chest.

'Ah, work is noble, but there is no position available.'

Phoebe had another of her bright ideas. She quickly explained her grand plan. 'The servants are emptying the first attic,' she finished. 'They are taking one piece at a time to the stables to be unwrapped and cleaned. Then the antiques come back into the house to be examined.'

'The forgotten treasures of a bygone generation make us meditate on the shortness of life and sigh,' the poet suggested dreamily.

'It makes one sigh for more space,' Phoebe retorted crisply. 'For storage is not the end of matters, as you will appreciate. Once the earl, and the dowager countess, have made a decision as to the fate of the items, some treasures will go back into storage, but others will need packing and crating, ready to be sold, and every single piece needs cataloguing.'

The poet looked horrified. Well, she had to have someone to help her, so she couldn't be too fussy, Phoebe reflected. He'd be all right if she told him what to do and kept an eye on him.

Phoebe turned to Robin as the courses changed. He had been eavesdropping and was laughing at her.

'I'm beginning to suspect that you are a managing young female, Miss Allen!'

'That sounds horrid!'

'Not at all! In fact, it's perfectly delightful when it results in a fine dinner like this one. However did you persuade Adolphe to turn out such decent food?'

'If I tell you, you'll have proof that I am indeed a managing female,' Phoebe laughed.

'Well there's been some management of the matter — I saw the blighter myself out on the gravel at the front of the house surrounded by all his trunks and a heap of copper pans. How did you persuade him not to leave? He seemed determined to go!'

That had been a horrific moment! Phoebe had felt her heart sink rapidly as she ran out to the front of the house to talk to the furious chef. Would Lady Chando be upset if the man actually left? Surely it wouldn't matter if he did leave? There must be better cooks to be found in England! Remembering how vile the previous evening's dinner had been gave Phoebe the confidence to call Adolphe's bluff, and he relented very quickly. And once he'd climbed down off his high horse and started talking to her, the situation was easy enough to resolve.

'Poor Adolphe,' she said to Robin.

'Melville had been forcing him to use inferior ingredients and he lost heart. I have promised to buy the best of everything and to discuss the menus with him every day.'

'I begin to see where the fellow got his reputation from now,' Robin said, vigorously scraping up the last of his vivid green watercress dish. 'Capital soup, what?'

Phoebe talked to Gordon-Rose again as she ate a meat dish of lamb's livers which was served hot and was perfectly cooked. When she turned back to Robin he was pink with awe.

'You are a bluestocking as well! Did I hear you spouting Greek to the poet?'

'I'm so rusty,' Phoebe sighed. 'Papa taught me Greek and Latin and we used to read the classics together, but I had no chance to use languages at the seminary.'

'I adore you, but you're far too clever for me,' Robin declared, looking at her with affection in his blue eyes. 'I'm glad that I got a warning off. I'd have spent my whole life trying to be intellectual enough for you. It would be frightfully wearing on a chap.'

Phoebe felt not only her cheeks but the back of neck going pink.

'A warning, about me?' she probed, trying to sound casual.

But Robin cast her a guilty laughing glance that suggested he'd realised his mistake and would let loose no more indiscretions.

'Only a few days now until hunting starts,' he laughed, firmly changing the subject. 'I can't wait! And you will be able to join us. I hear Felix is going to teach you to ride.'

10

No sooner had Phoebe finished breakfast the next morning than a knock at the door heralded Jenny and Miss Michaels. The dressmaker hurried into the room.

'Here is your new riding habit at last, Miss Allen. I'm so sorry it took such a long time to make.'

She shook out the most glorious cascade of teal-blue cloth. Each of the skirts was trimmed with piped navy cord, and the same navy piping ran around the collar, the pocket tops and all the seams. Although the design mimicked a Hussar's military uniform, the effect was enchantingly feminine.

'That is the most beautiful riding habit I've ever seen in my life!' Phoebe cried. 'But when will I wear it?'

Jenny smiled.

'Did you not know that a new horse

has arrived in the stables for you, Miss Allen? It's a cream mare, so I'm told, twelve hands high, just right for a small lady.'

Half an hour later Phoebe was lying on her back in a patch of prickly gorse bush, looking up at Felix's laughing face. He held out a hand to help her up.

'We'll make a horsewoman of you yet.'

'I'm glad you are finding it so funny!' complained Phoebe, rubbing her sore behind and brushing bits of furze from her beautiful habit.

Felix's smile lit up his face. She loved it when he stopped looking so serious and showed the lighter side of his nature.

'You've got a natural seat,' he said encouragingly. 'And she's got light hands, hasn't she, Spiller?'

She felt ridiculously proud of herself. It was strange how good his praise made her feel.

'Indeed she has, my lord,' agreed the groom, helping Phoebe back into the saddle. 'You'll be a cracking rider in no time.'

Felix wished that he hadn't noticed Phoebe's hands. She had beautiful hands: small, white, soft, and yet deliciously capable too. He kept wondering how they would feel against his skin, which was a troubling idea. He shook himself mentally. He might be prey to wicked images, but he didn't have to act on them. He could crush the pictures that were driving him wild. Or he should be able to; but somehow it wasn't that easy. He needed to get back to a calmer, more disciplined state of mind. He would return to the house.

'I'll leave you with Spiller,' he said brusquely.

But then a stable lad came running to say that one of the mares was foaling and Spiller was needed. Phoebe looked so disappointed that Felix heard himself saying, 'I'll stay with you, if you want to ride for a few minutes more.'

Her answering smile was so happy that his heart skipped a beat. And then two minutes later Phoebe fell off her pony again, and as he bent over her slight form and picked her up, his heart was thundering faster than it did before a battle. How was he going to keep his feelings locked up when he was holding her in his arms and inhaling her perfume? The smell of roses pushed everything out of his head. He wanted to kiss her until they were both dizzy, and that made her the worst person in the world for him to be with. With his background, he couldn't afford to be swayed by his feelings. Yet he held her longer.

'Have you hurt yourself?'

'No. I don't think so. I feel wobbly, though. Oh, my hand. I've cut it.'

'Show me!' Felix ordered.

Phoebe held out her hand, that beautiful soft white hand, and he caught it in his own so that he could examine it. The cut was tiny, but the touch of her skin made him ache for her. He bent his head and kissed the tiny wound.

Phoebe gasped when his lips touched her, and she snatched back her hand.

Felix took a step towards her. He hated the fact that she could make his control slip. He'd kept himself comfortably in check for years. It was Phoebe's fault that he'd lost it now. For a split second he hated her.

'Why so coy? Didn't you show me your hand so that I would kiss it better?'

Her grey eyes were wide open, the black lashes fluttering. He could read shock in them, and he hated himself for snapping at her. It was not her fault that his father had been an animal, or that she drove him crazy. He might have his blood, but he would not turn into the man he hated.

'Go back to the house now,' he growled.

The faintest tremor crossed her rosebud mouth, and his heart smote him. He should never have given way to anger.

'That's more than enough riding for

your first day,' he explained more gently. 'Little and often, that's the trick.'

The happier expression on her face made him feel better, although he meant to stay out of her way from now on. He had to stay away. The way she made him feel was dangerous. There was going to be an explosion if he didn't take care.

Despite her bumps and bruises, Phoebe found riding a horse to be an exhilarating experience. She told herself off for feeling disappointed that Felix didn't ride with her again. He was far too busy to spend his time giving her riding lessons. How could she want more when he'd given her a pony and the head groom always seemed happy to escort her around the estate?

Today, the sun shone brightly over the green of the parkland and the gold of the barley fields. The air smelled of apples, and for the first time Phoebe noticed a tinge of gold on the tops of the ash trees. Summer was waning.

'Smells like autumn,' Spiller pronounced. 'The nights will be drawing in soon.'

Phoebe reined in her cream mare.

'What is that dreadful building?' she asked.

They were riding over to the north-west side of the estate, in an area she had not yet visited. Plonked down in the middle of a wet-looking field was a ramshackle building. Marsh birds called overhead, making the scene feel lonely.

'That's the orphanage, Miss Allen. It's not been improved yet, so there's nothing to see.'

'I think I'll look at it anyway, Spiller, if you don't mind.'

The grubby-looking woman who shuffled to the door wasn't pleased when Phoebe announced that she meant to inspect the orphanage, and then found it filthy.

'Why don't you clean the place? You could get the children to help you.'

'Oh, my lady. I works my fingers to

the bone, but we can't afford cleaning. The price of soap is something terrible and you've no idea how much it costs to feed over thirty people.'

Phoebe raised her eyebrows and looked pointedly at the woman's green satin gown.

'As it happens, I know exactly how much it costs to feed and clothe foundlings.'

The woman's shifty gaze fell to the ground.

'You don't know how hard it is,' she whined.

'Oh, but I do,' Phoebe told her cheerfully. 'You can trust me to look into the matter of your funding but in return, I want you to make an effort with the cleaning. I will return next week to check on your progress.'

Back at Elwood, she hunted down Felix. She hadn't seen him alone since her riding lesson. If he was trying to avoid her, as he seemed to be doing, then she was too sensitive to run after him, but she wouldn't let pride stand in the way of the wellbeing of children. Today she had to track him down.

She found Felix in the stables. He was feeding carrots to a wild-looking, but utterly magnificent black stallion while Spiller and John Adam watched from a safe distance.

'What an incredible horse!' Phoebe gasped.

She tried to ignore the even more incredible man who was petting the horse. It was hard not to be charmed by Felix's beautiful green eyes, by the way he impatiently brushed his brown hair out of his eyes, and most of all by the smile that played over his generous mouth as he gentled the massive ebony stallion. You could see white rings around the horse's eyes and its nostrils flared red when it snorted. She couldn't bear to think of Felix getting hurt. She tugged at Spiller's sleeve.

'He's not going to ride that horse is he? It looks completely wild!'

Spiller smiled down at her.

'There isn't a horse alive that his

lordship couldn't ride if he had a mind to, but don't you worry. We keep Shaitan for breeding. His lordship's orders are that he's never to be ridden. He's got the devil in him all right. Taken chunks out of us all, he has.'

'Why do you keep such a vicious beast?'

'Because he's fast and so are his foals. They win races. People from all over England want their mares to breed with Shaitain.'

Hooves clattered as the stallion bucked and plunged. Phoebe felt her heart beating as she watched Felix masterfully leading the great beast towards one of the green paddocks. A lad scurried to open the gate and Felix let the horse plunge to its freedom. Then he turned, and walked back to the group. His face was unsmiling, grim even, and Phoebe's heart sank as he lifted a lazy eyebrow.

'Yes, cousin?'

As she explained about the orphanage, she could feel him distancing himself, she could see barriers in his eyes, but he was kind enough.

'Come with me to the office and John Adam will let you see the accounts. I have the orphanage on a list, of course, but I've been prioritising tasks that will return some revenue to the estate — you know how it is.'

Phoebe walked by his side as they left the stable yard and headed for the house. She suddenly made up her mind that he wasn't going to intimidate her.

'I know you have many demands on your time, but children are important. You cannot allow them to be neglected.'

And then her heart beat rather quickly as she waited for his response.

Felix couldn't help being amused by her attempt to tell him off. She was so tiny and so fearless that you couldn't help but admire her. And respect her, too. The expression in her grey eyes suddenly reminded Felix of his commanding officer. Colonel Peters was the kindest man he'd ever met, but he could be almighty sharp if he thought his officers were being stupid. He was glad, when he pushed open the door to the estate office, to find it empty.

'John Adam is away,' he remarked, and knowing what her response would be, he couldn't keep from teasing her. 'You will have to come back another day.'

'Surely you can find the details for me?' she demanded.

She had both hands planted on her hips. She was wearing a new brown riding habit with a red stock and the way she was gazing at him suddenly reminded him of a cheeky robin. He loved her perky expression and her sassy ways.

'Am I or am I not the master of this estate?' he grumbled, but he moved to obey her orders.

He watched as Phoebe ran a finger down the lines of figures. The tip of a very pink tongue showed between her lips as she concentrated. Then she looked up and met his gaze.

'The fault is in no way yours. You

have made the orphanage a generous allowance. I suspected the worst when I saw that woman's green satin dress. I may be wrong, it may be a simple case of mismanagement, but I wonder if she has been embezzling.'

Felix watched the pucker between her eyes and felt his heart melt. It was no good. He adored her. He nearly, nearly kissed her. It was fortunate that she placed the orphanage accounts on the table and moved away. It enabled him to take himself back into tight control, at least for long enough to make his escape.

'If the woman has been stealing, you may sack her. And now, I have urgent business, so if you will excuse me cousin . . .'

He could feel her staring after him but he refused to turn back. Today had only proved that he was right to keep away from her. Who would expect passion to flare over dusty books in the land agent's office? It was proof that any time he got close to her his control would slip. She was dangerous to his peace of mind.

* * *

A few days later Felix growled to himself as he tried to cross the marble hall. He had to dodge what seemed like every servant in the house as they scurried hither and thither, each carrying a mysterious load. The floor was so littered with boxes, bundles, and bags that it was impossible to see the black and white tiles. And then the most heart-rending howling startled him and completed the chaotic picture. He looked around, but could see nothing but the resident poet seated in fearful state at an old lectern in the centre of the muddle, solemnly and silently writing in a great ledger.

'What in the name of heaven is that noise?' Felix ejaculated.

The head footman padded towards him.

'Take a look in the music room,' Sam

bellowed, raising his voice above the howling.

Felix tried to take a step towards the music room, but his way was blocked by a pile of what looked like bronze breastplates and helmets from the English Civil War. He scowled at the heap of rusty armour.

'This looks like frightful chaos, Sam.'

'Miss Allen has the whole operation in hand. It's a pleasure to take orders from her if I may say so. She's a young lady as knows how many beans make five.'

'And the noise?' Felix enquired in long-suffering tones.

'Look in the music room,' Sam repeated, smiling.

As Felix entered the bright, wood-panelled room, the howling grew louder, but there was so much furniture that he had to peer around a collection of harps, look behind a gilt sofa, move aside six music-stands and step over at least five padded footstools before he got a clear view of Phoebe. She was sitting at the pretty, gilded harpsichord by the window, playing and singing. Little Pepe was under the instrument with his nose lifted to the heavens, howling.

Felix watched them, listening to Phoebe's song, enjoying the picture she made. Her dark green gown was beautifully framed by the crimson brocade curtains of the long windows. Despite the rain outside, the windows were open and the light fell on Phoebe's absorbed face. Then she seemed to become aware of him. She looked up, and stopped playing. Pepe stopped howling, but he continued to roll his eyes and look mournful.

'I'm so sorry. We are disturbing you. I thought you were at the sea gate.'

'Carry on,' Felix told her. 'It is nice to see the music room used, only, dare I suggest, that next time the beast be sent to the stables?'

Phoebe gave a gurgle of laughter.

'I had hoped to teach him to love music, but I do not appear to be convincing him.'

Felix regarded the shivering dog with aversion.

'You're keeping the Coopers' puppy? I can't say that I care for lap dogs. They do nothing but eat and yap.'

'It's how they are treated and trained,' Phoebe exclaimed indignantly. 'Pepe is as bright a little fellow as you could hope to meet.' She turned to the little dog.

'Come here, Pepe!'

The little dog came out from under the piano, looking more cheerful.

'Sit, Pepe!'

Pepe obeyed instantly, wagging his plumy tail.

Phoebe picked up a soft ball that had been lying on the floor near the piano. She rolled it gently to the other side of the room.

'Fetch, Pepe.'

A wide grin on his doggy face, Pepe scampered over to fetch the ball and ran back with it, dropping it obediently at her feet.

'You see?' she said to Felix, patting the dog. 'Your huntsman, Warren, is telling me how to go on. He knows a vast quantity about dog training. We are working on a new trick with Pepe. Let's see if he can remember it. If you would be so good as to stay perfectly still where you are.'

She picked up the ball and made Pepe walk with her to the other side of the room, then she gave the ball to Pepe, pointed at Felix and said commandingly, 'Deliver, Pepe!'

The little dog looked at Phoebe, grinning around his mouthful of ball. His tail wagged, but he made no move.

'Deliver, Pepe!' Phoebe said again. 'Take the ball to the earl.' She pointed at Felix. Pepe got to his feet, looked around the room in a bewildered fashion and sat down again.

Phoebe took the ball from him, laughing.

'He does not always manage his new trick. But, do you not think, sir, that it is unkind of you to call him stupid?'

Felix knelt down next to Pepe and the dog rolled over to have its tummy scratched. Its coat was healthy and glossy, and it regarded him from a bright brown eye brimming with intelligence and mischief. He'd under-estimated both its charm and intelligence, thought Felix, realising that he was won over.

The same way his mistress won me over, Felix thought. It was a shock, but as he looked at Phoebe he knew it was true. He gazed at her eyes, her face, her body, and thought that she was a beautiful person. His heart swelled with love, but at the same time a knot formed in his throat. It was difficult to put a name to the emotion he was feeling, and he was worryingly aware that it was not safe to feel it, or any emotion, but there was no doubt that it was real. He felt a sense of security and belonging when he looked at Phoebe, and he knew that he wanted her unconditionally. He didn't want to share her with anyone or anything. He wanted to touch her and kiss her and hug her and love her, but with another shock like ice water he knew that he dare not. He was afraid to let her in to his heart. He walked to the sound of his own drum, nobody else's. That way no one got hurt.

He jumped to his feet, and turned to leave, and then, aware that he was making a departure so abrupt that it could only be described as a rout, halted and spoke abruptly over his shoulder.

'I agree. He'll be a nice little beast, if he isn't spoiled.'

It wasn't what he had wanted to say, and he marvelled at the confusion in his emotions that he seemed to feel every time he spoke to Phoebe. His mood was not improved when he walked back into the hall and found the poet dithering in front of him. Gordon-Rose rolled his gooseberry eyes.

'Could you decide what to do with this silver epergne with elephants, and the matching candlesticks, well, all of the silver from India? There's a huge crateful of it. Shall we keep it?'

'Jupiter, no!' Felix said, feeling nothing but dislike for the thoroughly over-ornamented silver before him. 'I do not want to look at pepper pots crawling with palm trees and tigers.'

'That's what Miss Allen said you would say,' said the poet, exchanging the pepper pot for a mustard bowl that had snakes twined all around it and showing it the earl. 'But of course she told me to get a final opinion from you.'

'It's hard to believe an ancestor of mine had such vile taste,' Felix mused. 'You had better consult with my mother, however, as it was her uncle who brought this maharaja's delight back from the Orient.'

'She says that she prefers the Elizabethan silver and to get rid of anything with carved animals on it.'

'My sentiments exactly,' Felix said.

He suddenly became aware of hot breath around his ankles. He looked down. Two button-bright eyes laughed up at him. Pepe dropped the ball at his feet and sat smiling his doggy grin.

Felix had to smile.

'Very good, Pepe,' he said aloud, watching the plume of the dog's brown tail wag vigorously in response to the praise. 'Phoebe will have you trained in no time.'

Like the rest of us, he thought, as he made his way to his mother's room for his morning visit. He found his mother not just smiling, but beaming from ear to ear.

'Mama!' he ejaculated. 'It is fine to see you looking so well.'

The atmosphere was so different. Her room, although still cluttered, was clean and smelt fresh, and the glittering windows had been thrown open to allow in the scent of the sea.

'I haven't felt so well in a long time,' she confided. 'I worried when Phoebe said she was changing the menus, but I am astonished by how delicious the food has become.'

'Everyone has remarked upon the improvement.'

'Jenny tells me that Phoebe stood over the kitchen staff while they scrubbed every stone in the kitchen from top to bottom with boiling hot water, and she inspects it every day.'

'You don't mind, do you, Mama?'

'It is the greatest relief to me. While you were forced to exist on that miserable diet, I felt very conscious of my failings as a housekeeper.'

'Mama, there is no fault to find, with you or your housekeeping.'

'Not now, thanks to Phoebe. She has turned the whole place upside down, no that is not a fair description. She's like a mountain stream running through the house, clean and fresh and invigorating. I already cannot imagine being without her, and I cannot thank you enough for persuading her to visit me.'

'Turning the place upside down is a fair description for what is happening to the house,' Felix said, reminded of his errand. 'I came to ask you, Mama, are you being consulted? I should hate any item that you valued go to auction.'

'Do not worry, I am being shown every consideration. That nice young poet of Phoebe's is up here every hour on the hour, clutching his little list. I own I did not like the notion of a sale when you first broke it to me, but now I cannot think why. This house was built far too small compared with the castle.'

'Grandfather felt the cold. He once told me that he was miserable growing up in the freezing stone vastness of the castle and he was determined that the new house be small enough to warm.'

Georgiana smiled at her son and glanced around her cluttered room.

'I find that I am eager to have this room cleared out. It will appear far friendlier if it is furnished with a few suitable pieces. Imagine having room to move. I shall love it.'

'I will tell them to start work right away in your room.'

'Oh, no! Phoebe has a system and I dare you to meddle with it.'

'I dare not,' he said, smiling at his mother.

There was a bleating noise and a crash as a figure blundered into a stool behind them.

'How do you do, Miss Belmont?' Felix enquired politely. 'Are you quite recovered from your indisposition?'

'Indeed I am not!' she moaned. 'It is my nerves that have prostrated me, and only my affection for dear Lady Chando has led me to struggle from my bed of pain in order to remonstrate with you.'

Felix felt a familiar wave of exasperation as he looked at his mother's companion. She looked particularly ugly that day. The tip of her nose was an unbecoming pink, and the air of quivering hysteria that surrounded her was enough to make any man fear a feminine scene.

'My lord,' she continued, fixing her gooseberry-green gaze upon him and clasping her hands in front of her. 'You must stop this dreadful vulgar scheme. Not on my account, for I very well know that my feelings are of no importance, but do please consider your mother. Her sensitivities must be lacerated!'

'Indeed no, Thalia, you quite mistake the matter!' Georgiana insisted.

Miss Belmont's gooseberry eyes rolled wildly.

'Did you not say that society will consider us finished if we sell our household goods at public auction?'

'I must admit, I did. But since then I have reconsidered the matter and find the plan a good one.'

'It is not at all the thing!' Thalia's voice rose to a hysterical bleat. 'Only a low-down common mind could have produced such an improper scheme. I cannot bear to think of the seventh Earl of Chando holding a vulgar sale of goods. It is not to be borne! I dread to think of the gossip that will result.'

Felix had picked out the insult to Phoebe.

'Perhaps you would be more comfortable if you were to leave the house while this oh-so-improper, low-down common project is underway?' he suggested, and the mildness and gentleness of his tone was exactly the note that used to send his troops scurrying for cover faster than they fled from the enemy's fire. They all knew how dreadful the 'old man' could be when he was angry.

Thalia Belmont quivered all over as she registered his meaning. Her gooseberry eyes rolled in the direction of the dowager countess, but if she was waiting for Georgiana to beg her to stay, she was sadly disappointed. The dowager countess merely said gently, 'Dear Miss Belmont, I will of course lend you Jenny for the journey if you wish to leave us, but perhaps your nerves are upset and a little more rest will see you reconciled to the new plan?'

The companion gulped, put a hand to her throat and trotted away from them and out of the room. Felix's resolve to find a new home for Thalia Belmont crystallised at that moment.

'Do you think she will leave?' he asked hopefully.

'Where could she go?' his mother sighed.

11

A few days later the rose suite was ready and Phoebe and Kitty moved in. Phoebe was too ashamed to confess that she didn't like her new accommodation and wished she could return to the friendly comfort of the yellow room. The rooms in the rose suite, despite their undoubted loveliness, were totally intimidating by virtue of both size and grandeur. They also smelt of mice and were crammed to the rafters with the usual profusion of furniture, paintings, statues and knickknacks.

Kitty opened the door and scampered in.

'Here's another poem for you, Miss Allen.'

'Put it in the fire.'

'No, Miss Phoebe! It's lovely, all about flowers and such.'

'Gordon-Rose writes awful poetry,

and he's annoying me. I have told him not to send me any more drivel, and if he gives you any more scribbles I beg that you will put them straight on the fire.'

Kitty dropped the paper onto the log fire that burned in the stone hearth. She gave Phoebe a worried look.

'Are you feeling all right, miss?'

'I'm quite well, thank you, Kitty, and if I spoke sharply it was because the poet is driving me quite distracted.'

'He adores you, Miss Phoebe. It's ever so romantic.'

Kitty sighed, but Phoebe muttered, 'It's ever so infuriating,' under her breath. Gordon-Rose was a mixed blessing. At first he was baffled by the complexity of the task of sorting all the valuables in the house. Then, just as she was deciding that he would never get it, he suddenly grasped the whole system, even down to nuances of what could be sold and what must be kept for future generations.

'The earl has sixty-four great, great,

great, great grandparents, Miss Allen,' the poet had said. 'It took me a while to understand his family tree, but I'm clear now. I know what I'm doing with the family treasures; you can leave it to me.'

She still had to supervise him carefully, which was made harder by his open devotion to her. And it wasn't only the poet who was causing her pain. She was fighting with Jenny again. Kitty's entrance had interrupted their discussion, but Jenny was waiting and she had her arms folded in a manner that suggested she was feeling pretty determined.

Phoebe turned again to the grand dress laid out on her bed — a beautiful gown of striped silver silk in the latest mode.

'I won't wear it. It's a gorgeous dress, but surely it's a gown for a very grand occasion? The silk is so fragile, and look at the delicacy of the lace trimmings! I'm going to be busy all day. I'd feel terrible if I ripped it!'

The look in Jenny's hazel eyes was adamant.

'Your first obligation is to visit Lady Chando. You must wear appropriate clothing. Would you want the dowager countess to feel that she was not worth dressing up for?'

Once again, Phoebe submitted. Jenny slipped the lovely embroidered gauze over her head, nodding approvingly.

'That's right, Miss Allen. You'll soon get into the way of things.'

When she was dressed, Phoebe surveyed her exquisite reflection in the full-length looking glass. Behind her she could see the fantastic splendour of the rose room. She was living in unheard-of luxury with not one, but two faithful handmaidens to wait on her. So why wasn't she happier? She knew why, of course. Her heart was in a turmoil over Felix. He'd been so kind when they first met. She had no idea why he had gone all brooding on her. These days he seemed to walk in the shadows and she had no idea how to make the sunshine come back for them.

She had to force herself to sing as she tripped down the corridor to the countess's room. Pepe scampered along beside her, his little claws clicking on the fine polished floorboards, his jaws open in a doggy grin. Her overwhelmed mood passed off. Phoebe was nearly happy again. After all, there was plenty of good work to oversee, and the knowledge that she was being really useful at Elwood gave her a comfortable feeling of belonging in this very grand house.

'Here's my little songbird,' Georgiana said, smiling.

'I'm so happy! How can I not sing? But pray, if it is something a lady might not do, please tell me.'

'You do no harm with your singing, Phoebe! I like to hear it.'

'How can one not sing on such a beautiful day? It quite lifts the spirits after such a long spell of rain.'

'I have news that will make you happier yet. I have had word from

Eugenie. She is delighted to hear that your being here is turning out so well.'

'I owe her so much,' Phoebe said, smoothing her lovely dress.

'You have given her peace of mind,' Georgiana replied, a smile in her green eyes.

Phoebe sat next to the dowager countess, who took up her embroidery. A peaceful silence fell. Birds sang in the garden and a fresh green smell flowed into the room. The eyes of the two women met in a glance of perfect friendship. And then they heard a scurry in the passage outside, and Thalia Belmont's high bleating voice.

'She sounds excited,' the dowager countess said, her dark brows winging down.

Phoebe stood up.

'I'll leave you.'

'My dear, that's very sweet and tactful of you, but there's not the least need. Thalia will have to adjust to your being here.'

But it seemed that Miss Belmont had

a fresh grievance that was nothing to do with Phoebe.

'Those dreadful common Coopers are not leaving tomorrow as I expected.'

'They are Chando's guests,' Georgiana said reprovingly. 'He wishes them to stay longer.'

'Leeches!' snapped Miss Belmont.

For once Phoebe was in agreement with Thalia Belmont. She hated the idea of Alicia staying longer. She had to struggle with her conscience before she could say calmly, 'They are very pleasant company. I think Felix finds Mr Cooper's advice of great use to him in business matters.'

Miss Belmont snorted.

'I think Mrs Cooper means to sell her daughter. The pretensions of some people! It just shows how vulgar tradespeople are, thinking that money can buy them a good name.'

Thalia had clearly forgotten that Georgiana's family had been in manufacturing, but Phoebe hadn't.

'Alicia is sweet and beautiful,' she

cried warmly. 'If Felix should care for her, it would be a very suitable match.'

A light touch on her hand told her that Georgiana appreciated Phoebe's attitude, but Phoebe's heart twisted insider her. She couldn't bear to think of Felix marrying Alicia, yet the very fact that he'd asked the Coopers to prolong their stay suggested that he might be considering her as his bride. Phoebe felt so distraught at the idea that she could no longer hide the fact that she had fallen deeply in love with him. Well, she might have admitted the truth to herself, but her love would have to remain secret from the world. Despite her resolve to control her feelings, tears stung her eyes. She could no longer fool herself. She loved him.

'Phoebe, are you ill? You have gone white as a sheet.'

'I'm fine. Isn't it time we set off for church?'

The Abbey of Saint Bees was no more than a small cluster of grey stone buildings and a stone church with tall pine trees growing behind it. A heavy rain had fallen earlier, but it had stopped now. Silver drops hung on the grass and the gravestones, and the air was fresh. The vicar took the service with great dignity and compassion.

As everyone left the church, Mrs Cooper refused to get into the first carriage.

'Do sit by my daughter, my lord. I'm sure you and Alicia will find lots to talk about.'

Mr Cooper tugged at her arm.

'Don't embarrass the man!' he hissed.

But Felix wasn't embarrassed, or trapped. He hardly seemed to be directing events but Robin jumped in beside Alicia. Robin's blond head bent to Alicia's and they appeared to be exchanging a secret as the horses broke into a trot and carried them away. Felix watched them go with a smile in his eyes. A second carriage whisked Mr and Mrs Cooper away before they could complain.

Another carriage drew up beside them. Felix offered a hand to Phoebe, but she hesitated. He examined her face, his green eyes gentle.

'What is it?'

Phoebe's heart melted at his kindness, and she felt able to confide in him. She cast a wistful glance over the sheep-nibbled turf of the cliffs to the line of blue-grey water that sparkled beyond it.

'Could we look at the sea? I have never seen it properly.'

He gestured to the carriage to wait, and they walked a few yards to a point where it was possible to view the coastline. Sea gulls called above them. The tide was in, and the twinkling water seemed to move for miles in every direction.

Phoebe's lips parted. She felt the wind in her hair, on her cheeks. The fresh smell of the sea lifted her heart. Vast clouds of all shapes and sizes, in all shades of grey, black and white, raced across the horizon and massed over the silver sea.

Felix gestured to the left and to the right.

'Morecambe Bay is that direction, the Lake District is over there.'

'It's beautiful,' Phoebe said, gazing at a piece of broken rainbow.

She felt Felix's companionship, and it comforted her. Without looking she knew that he was waiting for her with gentleness and patience. Even though they were physically standing apart, his goodwill crossed the space between them and, as she returned to the carriage, she marvelled at the strength that came from him.

Dinner that night was a merry affair. Robin had been placed next to Phoebe, but she noticed that he couldn't take his eyes off Alicia. She looked less nervous this evening and the light from the long windows showed off her creamy white skin and beautiful green dress.

'Lovely!' Robin said.

She knew she had to tell him off,

despite feeling a cold pain around her heart.

'And taken,' she said, firmly. 'She's to be engaged to your best friend.'

Except for meals, she never saw the woman. Alicia seemed to spend most of her life yawning on a sofa in the morning room or in trotting around after her mother. She didn't seem to take part in the life of the house, but there she indubitably was. All the colour and fun went out of the evening. It was an effort to smile at her companion.

'People say she's trying to marry Chando,' Robin was saying now, with the openness that seemed to characterise him, 'but I can't believe it's true. Felix runs away from wedding bells faster than any man I've ever met.'

'But he must marry sometime.'

'He says never, and I believe him. It's a perfect obsession with him.'

'Why?'

'It's not for me to say.'

She appreciated the fact that he wouldn't gossip about Felix.

'I wish I knew him better, but you are right to respect his confidence. You are a good friend, Robin.'

He looked down at her with affection in his eyes.

'Nobody knows him well. He keeps his feelings to himself. But you are family, Phoebe, so I will tell you that he had a rough time with his father, and that's the root of the issue.'

'So that's why he doesn't let people close,' Phoebe murmured.

'He'll never marry,' Robin repeated.

'Poor Alicia.'

'I'm sure she doesn't care for him. I think the match was her parents' idea. Still, to make you happy, I won't think of Alicia any more, not unless Chando says I may. I shall ask him if he would mind if I courted the girl. I could do with a rich wife, if I could find one who wouldn't care that I am the youngest son, or who wouldn't be frightened away by my eccentric family.'

'I am sure your family are delightful,' Phoebe said primly.

Robin promptly regaled her with such funny stories about the eccentricities of the Hathaway family that a quarter of the details couldn't possibly have been true.

'I cannot believe that anyone would go hunting on a big black bull,' she told him.

'It's true! Great-great grandfather simply hated horses! And his son invented a musical toothbrush because he hated the sound of bristles scraping. All the Hathaways have had bees in their bonnets about one thing or another.'

Phoebe knew that Robin was the youngest son in a family with a lineage that stretched back to Charlemagne, but with no money whatsoever. Robin was so nice that he deserved a rich wife. She'd love to see him marry Alicia.

The men didn't seem to spend long over their port and cigars that evening. They soon filed into the library, and Phoebe vowed to have at least eighty percent of the furniture taken out the next day, for there was hardly room to breathe. It was full of broad shoulders. Just as everyone was settling down with a cup of tea, Pepe barked for admittance at the door. Phoebe blushed, and gestured to Ruben to let him in.

The splendidly-attired footman bowed and held open the door with a stately flourish so that the tiny King Charles spaniel could make his grand entrance. Pepe paced in, his long ears flowing, his little paws lifted high. The men shouted with laughter, and even Mrs Cooper smiled.

'Look at the dear little doggie,' she said, seeming not to realise that this was the very dog she had found wanting as a fashion accessory and ordered to be destroyed.

Mr Cooper's smile was derogatory.

'What do women see in these walking muffs?'

Phoebe remembered that Mr Cooper was a guest and bit her tongue.

Felix spoke up, surprising her.

'He's the most intelligent little beast. Show off his tricks, Phoebe.'

Pepe sat, died for the king and begged for a biscuit with such charm that everyone clustered around to watch him and Mr Cooper apologised for calling him stupid.

'Does he know any more tricks?'

'Do you have a something that he can deliver for you?' Phoebe asked.

'Here, take this cigar tube,' Mr Cooper said. His laughing glance slid around the room and landed on his wife. 'Would Pepe deliver it to the charming lady in crimson?'

Phoebe pointed at Mrs Cooper and said, 'Deliver, Pepe, deliver!'

The little dog looked at Mrs Cooper, spat out the cylinder and growled, lifting his upper lip to show white teeth as he snarled! Mrs Cooper's face contorted and the room fell silent. Phoebe was aghast, and for once she couldn't think of a thing to say to retrieve the situation. Felix moved forward, smiling at the watching faces.

'The little chap is even more intelligent that we supposed. He knows perfectly well that cigars are not suitable for ladies! Here, Pepe, deliver the cigar to Robin instead.'

The atmosphere eased at once. Phoebe felt so impressed by the way he'd handled the problem. When Felix was around, she didn't have to worry about anything because she could trust him to solve any situation. Pepe threw Felix a laughing glance, picked up the cigar tube and took it to Robin. The burst of laughter and applause that followed his trick didn't seem to faze him at all. The vigorous wagging of his tail suggested that he knew how clever he had been.

That night, Felix and Robin stayed up after everyone else had retired. The footman made up the fire and brought them a bottle of brandy and some water. The two friends drew up chairs to the fire that blazed in the stone hearth, stretched out their long legs, and smoked in companionable silence for a while.

Robin blew out a plume of smoke and watched his friend's face closely.

'I am sorry that you have warned me off the little songbird. She is quite out of the ordinary. She's like a fresh mountain stream.'

'She has no money,' Felix replied, somewhat icily.

'What a shame. I fell for Miss Allen the moment I met her. She's a taking little thing, and jolly pretty with those big grey eyes of hers and I've always been a fool for dark curls. Yes, she's bang up to the mark in every respect! But, if she's poor it cannot be. You know my situation, Chando. I have to marry money. I must be able to support my mother and sisters. The old man left us nothing — and you know how that is! I would marry one of the gorgons if she had enough money.'

Felix stirred in his chair. His eyes opened very wide as his gaze fell on his friend.

'What?' Robin enquired.

'Alicia Cooper needs a husband.'

'Oh,' Robin said, cautiously. 'But am I not to understand that she, that you and she . . . '

Felix shrugged, and kicked one of the glowing logs with the toe of his boot.

'I wish you all the luck in the world in finding a rich wife.'

Robin brightened at once.

'How much will she get when she marries? Come on, don't curl your top lip at me. How much?'

'Fifty thousand a year, and she's an only child so one day the whole Cooper empire will be hers.'

'Tally ho!' muttered Robin.

And his eyes remained thoughtful even as the talk turned to the subject of horse breeding.

12

Felix went through the great hall and out of the main entrance, and then he walked around the house, enjoying the mild air of a warm, grey October day. The lavender walk lay on the south side of the house. Down the side of the path ran a line of topiary box trees clipped into the shape of elephants. He'd loved their flapping ears and lifted trunks when he was a boy. He rounded the corner and smiled as he saw the topiary creatures. The row of green elephants still impressed him. The trees had been growing in size and splendour since Felix last took notice of them.

A thrush in a magnolia tree sang loudly as he walked towards the sound of laughter. There was Phoebe, pretty in a soft-blue morning dress, there was a well-groomed donkey with a fluffy coat and shining hooves, and there, in a brand-new wicker invalid carriage, was his mother laughing and looking as well as he'd ever seen her.

Phoebe seemed to sense his approach and turned her smiling face towards him, her eyes very silver in the outside light.

'Only think, it is years since your mother saw these darling elephants!'

As Felix looked into Phoebe's eyes, the smell of the lavender seemed to fill his nose and clear his brain. He realised how dear she was to him. How much he loved her. How difficult his life now was. The notion of love had been easy to cast aside before he'd met Phoebe. Secure in his masculine independence he'd thought he cared nothing for having a wife. It was true that he didn't want to behave like his father, but it had been easy for him to foreswear love because he hadn't been able to understand why men wanted to marry. It was accepted as truth in the gentlemen's clubs that men who married lost their independence and their freedom. What rubbish! He would lose nothing in an alliance with Phoebe. He'd be the richer for her company.

He realised that he thought about her all the time and that he wanted her to think about him. Her image captured his senses to such an extent that he couldn't analyse exactly how she made him feel, but he knew now that a lovely woman was the most glorious being in the world. She was a precious jewel and a wicked enchantress. She was gentle and loving, she was clever and managing, she was sweet and tactful, and she was pert and snippy, and he didn't know which side of her he preferred the most. She was all he could ever dream of, yet he couldn't afford to give in to his feelings. What kind of a man was he if he cast aside all his promises the very first time he met temptation? A vow was worthless until it was tested, and he reminded himself bitterly, he was sworn to self-control.

'Isn't the donkey adorable,' Phoebe cried. 'Look at her chocolate muzzle and her furry ears.'

'Stubborn brutes,' Felix said. He had to swallow and try to improve the rough sound his voice made. 'We had no end of trouble with them on campaign.'

Phoebe seemed to notice nothing amiss. She was her usual composed and merry self.

'Well if you will drag the poor beasts all over rocky, snowy mountains and let them be shot at I should think they would rebel!' She kissed the donkey's nose. 'Primrose gives us no trouble at all. She loves pulling Lady Chando around, doesn't she, Spiller?'

The head groom smiled and Felix marvelled at Phoebe's magic. Only charms and spells of a most advanced nature could have persuaded his grumpy huntsman to spend time training a lap dog, and his head groom to procure and lead a donkey! And he had to admit the results were splendid. A soft rose colour bloomed in his mother's cheeks and her whole face was alive with enjoyment.

'I'm having a wonderful time, thanks

to Phoebe. My dear, could we take a turn as far as the mermaid fountain? The lily pool was my favourite place to sit when I came here as a bride.'

'Tomorrow,' Phoebe promised, smiling affectionately into the green eyes. 'Today has been very successful, but it is the first day you have been out, and you mustn't get tired.'

Felix clenched his fists as he watched them return to the house. It was so hard to be near Phoebe. He must be cool. He must stay distant. Yet as soon as he got near her, he wanted to laugh and make love to her. He knew he couldn't trust himself. One laughing glance from Phoebe's eyes and all his self-control would melt. There was only one thing for it. Somehow he would have to create a distance between himself and his love. Could he bear to pretend that he was angry with her? Could he somehow make her so angry with him that she would stop smiling at him? No, he couldn't bear it. He'd simply have to stay out of her way instead.

Phoebe noticed that Felix was keeping out of the house, but she kept herself busy having the attics turned out. A mountain of saleable treasures was revealed, and every piece had to be cleaned, catalogued and packed. Robin, who had received a letter from his mother summoning him to a family wedding in London, agreed to supervise the removal of the first load of auction items and liaise with Christie's in Pall Mall. Lawyer Caldicott had advised them to hire a warehouse in town and, in order not to alarm the many, many people who were owed money, not to begin selling until all was catalogued and they were ready to proceed.

'For we do not wish to create the impression that the estate is in difficulties, and it would be impossible to meet our obligations if everyone demanded his money in a panic,' he said in his dry way.

'But we'll have to pay storage costs,'

Phoebe demurred. 'Surely people will trust Chando to pay them?'

Felix, who had somehow found himself unable to pass the library door without walking in to stand next to his darling, nodded to the lawyer.

'Tell her the sum total of our debts.'

The lawyer pursed his lips and whispered the frightful sum.

Phoebe's cheeks went perfectly white. Felix nodded at her shocked expression.

'I will own to some sleepless nights,' he admitted.

'You have contrived amazingly well,' was all that she said to him, but the look of high admiration that lit her grey eyes made him feel like a king.

What a dangerous feeling! Felix whirled on his heel and stalked out, cursing the weakness that meant he couldn't stay away from her. Yet he had to admit that her approval was as good as a medal, and the feeling that she looked up to him was as sustaining as the delicious dinners that were now the norm at Elwood. It wasn't hard to agree with John Adam that evening when he turned to Felix and smiled.

'Miss Allen is a wonder,' that good man declared, taking a sip of fine wine from a sparkling glass.

The inhabitants of Elwood were sitting at the clean polished dinner table in a freshly refurbished room. The crimson curtains were drawn back, allowing in the light. The ornate Indian whatnots had vanished, and the plain silver in use sparkled and shone. The whole party was tucking into delicious crispy duck with fresh new green peas. The land agent took a greedy mouthful before continuing.

'I took a look at the inventory of items to be sold. She assures me that the estimates are conservative, but I tell you frankly, my lord, that if all the reserves are met, you'll not only free the land, but there'll be enough for investment as well.'

'We must ask Hans van de Mayer to return from Holland.'

'Another windmill and a few more drainage cuts would soon pay for themselves. Gosforth Farm is running over half as many sheep again since we started pumping water out of the fields.' The agent nodded, smiling. 'We could give a bit of thought to improving our beef herd as well. What would you say to a champion bull?'

Mr Cooper joined in the conversation.

'There's a good seam of coal running out to sea at the Dalton mine. You could afford to shore up the tunnels and re-open the mine.'

Felix liked that idea. 'Yes, that would create jobs and that would please the local people.'

'Why not let me arrange a canal consortium? If you had a spur of waterway that ran down to your land, you could get coal to the Midlands at a quarter of the price.'

By the time the port had gone around, their wish list was a long one.

'We'd better hope Miss Allen keeps

weaving her magic!' John Adam said, smiling, as they went to join the ladies in the now charming and comfortable library.

Felix's happy mood crumbled when he saw that Miss Belmont was waiting to pounce.

'I have information of a most alarming nature to impart,' she bleated, tossing a white scarf over her shoulder.

Felix met the goggling green gooseberries of her eyes and wished her at Jericho.

'Indeed?' he enquired, politely.

She leaned closer. Too close. He took a step back.

Felix wondered how it was that a middle-aged lady could be more unpleasant to deal with than a military attack.

'Those dreadful Coopers have put off their leaving date again!' she screeched. 'You will have to be firm. It's the only way to deal with such common upstarts. I'm beginning to think they will never leave.'

Miss Belmont's voice rose high in her agitation and Alicia overheard. She hung her head miserably and the hands in her lap twisted and trembled.

Phoebe marched over to the unhappy girl at once. She sat down beside her and put her arm around her waist.

'We enjoyed the Coopers' company so much that we begged them to stay,' Phoebe told Miss Belmont.

Her grey eyes were flashing as she faced the complaining companion.

Felix felt his heart swell to twice its normal size. Ah, she was beautiful. How could he not be charmed? It wasn't just her grey eyes, or her creamy face with the arching eyebrows that complemented her beautifully dressed dark curls. It was the genuine goodwill in her smile as she championed Alicia that Felix found irresistible. Imagine if he'd never met her!

He had to blink hard as he thought how lucky he was to know her. He had to blink even harder when he remembered that he must avoid her. He cursed the fact that he had his father's blood. It was all very well swearing that he'd never run wild, that he'd never hurt anyone, but wasn't the very violence of his feelings about Phoebe proof that he was a passionate man?

He was tempted to say that love was a natural feeling and it was safe to allow passion in to his life, but what if this were the first step to becoming like his father? What if he were to become ill or suffer bad fortune? Would his resolve crumble further? Would he succumb to the next temptation and the next, until he became as uncontrolled in his manner as his father had been? He couldn't take the risk.

It was no use wishing for things that he couldn't have. He could no more marry Phoebe than he could have stayed in the army. Life was not fair, and his personal feelings came second to his duty. He must keep his distance, he must avoid her, but it was hard for him to turn away, knowing that she was watching him, wondering why he was avoiding her.

Later that night Phoebe washed in cool water and then slipped on a long rose-coloured nightdress. She thought of Miss Belmont first. The silly woman was jealous, frightened and unhappy. If only she could understand that it was all wasted emotion. Of course the Coopers were enjoying their stay as an earl's guest in a stately home, who wouldn't? But why should Miss Belmont resent it? No matter how many visitors they had, neither Georgiana nor Felix would hear of turning out a relation.

Phoebe got into her oaken four-poster bed. It was four feet high and it was six feet wide, and she felt like a pea in a twenty-acre field as she curled up in the Irish linen sheets. The autumn night was warm, so the floor-length curtains of palest pink silk embroidered all over with Chinese roses were drawn back to allow in the fresh air. She snuggled into the heap of luxurious goose-down pillows, all covered in the finest linen cases, but she could not sleep. An hour or two later, she gave up.

'Too much tea and excitement just before bed,' she muttered, throwing back the linen sheet and climbing out.

She put on a flowing wrap of the finest lace. It was dyed a darker pink than the rose-coloured nightgown and gave a delicious layered effect. She felt like a princess in a fairy-tale as she crossed the room and curled up in the window seat. It was cool by the open windows; in fact it was downright refreshing: the cold air made Phoebe hug her feet to her and wrap her arms around her knees.

Pepe stirred, and his bright eyes turned in her direction. He jumped out of his basket, his tail wagging as he scampered over to her and curled up on her knee. She cuddled his warm body and thought of Felix. She had been trying not to, she really had, but the situation with Robin and Alicia was raising eager hopes in her heart. Surely, surely she was not mistaken. Robin was making every effort to win Alicia over, and Felix was positively encouraging him! Mrs Cooper may still be hoping to marry her daughter to an earl, but she suspected that Mr Cooper had no such illusions. He was staying because he liked Robin, and Felix was happy to have him because the businessman's knowledge was of real help to him.

The elation she felt when she realised that Felix was trying to get rid of his prospective fiancée made her realise that she wasn't a nice person at all. She wanted Felix for herself. Whenever they were together everything else in the world fell to a hazy background. Earlier that evening instead of making an excuse and moving away as he usually did Felix had ended up sitting by her and his reserve had seemed to melt for a precious hour.

They had a great conversation, not about feelings of course. The whole world could have listened in and heard nothing wrong in their words, but what a current had run between them. There was nothing so sweet as the satisfaction she had felt while they were talking, even when they disagreed. And wasn't it amazing how much they had to say, about little nothings as well as the major task of saving the estate? As soon as Phoebe stopped to take a breath, Felix picked up, and the instant he stopped she took up the conversation. She could barely remember what they had talked about. It didn't matter. It was the meeting of two souls.

And all the time, Alicia had been laughing with Robin while Felix smiled his approval. Don't get too excited! Phoebe warned herself, but still she watched Alicia's smiles and animation with growing enthusiasm, and every fibre of her being was praying that Robin would manage to carry her off. And that would leave Felix free to do, what, exactly? On the one hand there was no doubt that he was encouraging Robin, yet on the other, his manner with her was so odd. One minute he'd be smiling and seeming to love being with her, the next second he was retreating into a chilly remoteness. What could he be thinking? She understood him a little better after her conversation with Robin. It explained the sadness in his eyes. Given his childhood, she could understand why he avoided feelings. He clearly wasn't going to confide in her, so it was going to be up to her to find out what was going on in his head. Whether he liked it or not, she was going to make him talk.

Pepe stiffened in her arms, gave a sharp yip, and looked out of the window. She could smell mushrooms and crisp autumn leaves, and she now saw yellow lamplight and heard voices over towards the stables. There must be a problem with one of the horses. She was so wide awake that she might as well go and see if she could be of any help.

It was dark outside and the bulk of the house hid the light that she had seen from her window. She was just wishing that she'd brought a candle when she saw a flicker of movement. She crashed to a halt and felt ice in her stomach. Was that a shadow, or a man? She glanced down at Pepe but he continued walking, completely unconcerned. Animals had better senses than humans. It must be a shadow. She took two more steps, and the shadow reached out and grabbed her. Fingers closed tightly around her upper arms. The shock of the contact drove everything from her mind but primeval fear, a feeling that was swiftly followed by a feeling of rightness. The moon popped out from behind some dark clouds, casting silver light on the scene, but she already knew who it was.

'Chando!' she breathed, feeling his presence invading the night scene, taking it over, leaving no room for anyone else in her mind.

'What are you doing?' he demanded.

'I was going to see if they needed help in the stables!' she whispered.

His grip did not slacken.

'There is no need. All is well now, thank you. We have another fine foal.'

He did not let her go. They were both breathing in short, shallow breaths, as if they had been running. Heat shimmered in the air around them, working its magic once more. Their bodies came together in a crush, fitting perfectly. Phoebe's arms flew around his neck, and when she felt the force of his arms, reaching out to enfold her, she let out a small cry of pleasure. She knew he was going to kiss her, and she also knew that she wasn't going to stop him. It was what she had been wanting, but it was also what she had feared.

'You distract me so,' he growled, 'that I have no idea what I'm supposed to be doing.'

And he reached out and captured her lips, kissing her where no one but he had ever kissed her before. His kiss was so many things: heat, satisfaction, unbearable provocation, excitement, security, danger. An inner demand rose insistently in Phoebe; she had to kiss him back. She had to feel the heat of his lips as she, as she, well, to be truthful, as she encouraged him and wanted him right back. Being an active partner in a kiss was heady, exciting. She soared to the heavens.

'Ah,' she breathed, 'you make me feel . . . '

'What?' he whispered. 'Tell me what I do?'

She could feel his large hands, spread over her shoulders, drawing her to him.

'You make me shiver,' she gasped against his neck. 'Can you not feel me?'

'I feel you,' he said, his voice deep and husky. 'You are soft and warm and utterly sweet and desirable.'

And his lips touched hers with a gentleness that only sharpened the desire that flowered inside her.

'You have my heart!' he added.

His words shocked and thrilled her with a delicious zing. Did he mean it? She took a shaky breath and looked at his face, trying to read the strong planes of his features. He looked back, examining her soul in the moonlight. The love she felt for him was mutual to go by the way he was looking at her now. There was a softness in his eyes that tempted her to try to get him to open up to her.

'Felix,' she began.

He took Phoebe's hand. His skin was warm and vital on hers.

'Come inside,' he breathed.

She followed him. Shaking, trembling, frightened of she knew not what. The kitchen was still silent, still dark save for the glow of the banked fire. Phoebe would have moved forward, but Felix captured her in his arms from behind and breathed in her ear, sending shivers down her spine.

'Keep still.'

A circle of yellow light appeared in the passage and bobbed towards them. It was one of the kitchen maids. Yawning she put her candle on the long, scrubbed pine table. She opened the black iron door of the stove and began to stir up the coals. Phoebe could feel the heat of Felix's body all down her spine. It was shockingly intimate.

The maid picked up the candle and crossed the flagstone floor to enter one of the small pantries. The kitchen fell dark. Phoebe blinked. She could see nothing. Exposure to the light of the candle had destroyed her night vision. Felix pushed her forward. Hand in hand, they moved silently across the kitchen, slipped through the shadowy passage and entered the dark main hall.

'Careful,' warned Felix.

As if she didn't know how cluttered and strewn with antiques the hall was! At the foot of the stairs they paused. The shadowy dark was frustrating. She couldn't see his eyes, but, after that kiss, surely there was a tender feeling between them that would allow her to speak.

'Are you friends with me, Felix?'

'What do you think?' was his soft reply. His voice was lingering, deep, intimate, and husky.

'Only, you keep avoiding me.'

His tone became sharp, cold, and harsh.

'So?'

'Can't you tell me why?'

'No!'

The colder his voice became, the sorrier she felt for him. Oh, if only she could see his eyes.

'I don't want to talk about it,' he growled.

She felt as if she'd been punched in the heart. A silence fell between them while Phoebe tried to form her next question,

'But you kissed me . . . ' she blurted out. 'You shouldn't kiss me if you won't talk to me.'

And then she could have kicked herself for telling him off. It wasn't what she meant to say at all. But it was true, and her own feelings were swelling within her.

'You will not openly share your feelings with me, yet you kiss me when nobody is looking. What am I to think?' she cried softly.

'I shall never speak to you or kiss you again. You want more than I am prepared to give you!' he growled. 'If you push me and push me then my control will snap, and there will be a disaster.'

And he turned and left her.

Phoebe gave a soft choked cry of frustration. She waited for him to turn back, to look over his shoulder and whisper something that would both put her fears at rest and acknowledge that he'd just kissed her senses to oblivion. After all that had happened, surely he could not simply mount the marble staircase, tread by noiseless tread, and leave her standing in the dark. She held her breath and waited.

But that's exactly what he did. No smile, no touch, no word to reassure her. Not a single syllable to say about how and why he'd kissed her. Phoebe blinked into the empty darkness. Her heart felt sore.

'Well, if that's the way you want it,' she fumed. 'Don't think I want to speak to you, either.'

Anger fizzed as she returned to her room, but it soon drained away leaving her to face the truth. She did want to speak to him and she did want to understand him, but until she understood him better she was going to back off, but only temporarily. She was stronger than he thought and she was going to find out why he was resistant to any kind of relationship.

13

Over the week that followed, Phoebe was astonished by how blind people could be. Not one person in the house seemed to notice that she and Felix were not speaking! Oh, of course they conversed, with painful politeness, over the packing and the inventory, but nothing more. How could people not sense the frost in him? His green eyes were cold and remote when he spoke to her. He held his body stiffly, as far away from her as it was possible to stand and still be heard. His words trickled grudgingly from between thin lips. Stubborn, stubborn Felix!

She missed him! She yearned to return to the previous days when they had been more in accord and she had been so happy. Life was pale without him. It was Felix who had been putting a song on her lips and a smile in her heart. She missed their chit chat, their growing warmth, the way he always seemed to be on her level, but first one week and then a second crawled by, and neither of them relented a bit.

Because Felix was busy about the estate, Georgiana asked Phoebe if she would help to interview the new major domo. It took only took five seconds to dismiss the first candidate.

'Far too grand and proper,' Phoebe whispered as the man left.

The second candidate fared no better.

'Too weak and insubstantial,' she declared.

The next candidate was called O'Neil, and hailed from Ireland.

'I noticed that you are packing. Does it mean that I will be expected to travel with the family?'

Phoebe shook her head.

'We are merely selling a few unwanted items.'

She had tried to speak as if selling the family belongings were a normal thing to do, but for a split second, the prospective major domo looked surprised. Georgiana smiled.

'I want the clutter all gone, every bit of it.'

'You must leave some valuables for your descendents,' Phoebe argued.

'I no longer wish to be surrounded by junk.'

O'Neill watched them bickering for a few moments, then offered to devise a rotation system.

'We could store the valuable items, and display a few at a time.'

Eyes met and they all nodded. O'Neil took up his new duties immediately, and with him in charge the house seemed to run itself and Phoebe felt as if she were no longer needed in the same way. She found herself in unexpected sympathy with Miss Belmont's hurt feelings, for O'Neil joined with Georgiana in shutting out Phoebe from the house completely, shooing her out to ride in the sunshine.

Still, it was such a pleasure to gallop

on her cream pony (yes, she could gallop now) over the hills and over the moors and one never-to-be-forgotten day along the sands of the beach, that she didn't much mind being sent out, and it also meant that she had more time to spend at the orphanage. There had been no need to dismiss the lady in the green dress. Once she realised that Phoebe meant to call in regularly and that she could no longer dip into the housekeeping, the woman vanished into the night, fleeing across the marshes never to be seen again.

John Adam was advertising for somebody new, but until an appointment could be made, Phoebe was making sure that the children were looked after. Under her care, the children rapidly put on weight and greeted Phoebe with smiling rosy faces every time she visited.

A few days later a letter came from Robin. It was a good letter, very like Robin himself. Phoebe wished he was back at Elwood. Maybe he'd act as a buffer between her and Felix! He wrote that he had rented a perfectly enormous warehouse, and the first wagon load of sale items had arrived safely. 'Phoebe was right,' he wrote. 'The chaps from Christies drooled over that pile of junk! The rustier it was, the more they seemed to like it!' Seeing as the items were so valuable, he'd taken the liberty of appointing a couple of watchmen, old soldiers, he assured them, from Felix's own regiment. He also said that his cousin's wedding feast had gone very well, and that although he had business to see to before he could leave home, he was hoping to return to Elwood by the mail coach within the next couple of weeks.

'He'll come back soon. There's nothing to keep him at home,' said Felix who had unbent slightly as they shared the letter.

'What is his mother like?' Phoebe asked, curious.

Felix pulled a face.

'Think of a codfish,' he advised. 'He

was a late surprise, and she has never forgiven him for being born.'

She couldn't help laughing.

'But Robin's so lovely,' she protested, thinking of his smiling face, his cheerful ways and endless good nature.

She'd spoken too impetuously. Felix's green eyes shadowed then went frosty and he stalked away. Phoebe stared after him, feeling a cold hard lump forming in her throat. Why was Felix being so hateful? Could he be jealous? If he was it would mean that he cared, but if he cared, then why wasn't he speaking to her? Could it be that *she* was causing the tension that fizzed between them and making it hard for him to converse? She resolved to act differently. This very day she would speak to him, calmly, casually, and in a friendly manner, something about the weather, perhaps, any remark to get them chatting again. She couldn't bear this coldness between them.

Talking to him was easier said than done. She tried hard to speak to him in private, but, although she trailed him into every room in the house that day, and even stalked after him into the stable yard, it was impossible to get a moment alone. There was always someone talking to him on estate business. As Felix joined the group in the library that evening, Phoebe stood by the crackling log fire and felt her mouth dry. She swallowed hard, closed the few steps between them, opened her mouth, and then closed it again as Miss Belmont stood up and clapped her hands.

'Everyone! Gordon is going to read us one of his lovely poems.'

Gordon Gordon-Rose flicked his long fringe and stared hard at Phoebe with his prominent gooseberry eyes.

'Ah, the sun to my moon!

'Phoebus is gold, clad like the daffodils . . . '

It was excruciating! Phoebe writhed as the poet went on declaring his love in terrible verse. Somewhere around the tenth stanza, after much repetition and many references to his inspiration, Miss

Belmont suddenly realised that she was listening to a paean to the woman she considered an interfering interloper. Her gooseberry eyes flew wide open and she sat upright in outrage.

'Well I never! That's enough poetry for now, Gordon!'

Felix had understood the poet's intentions from the first line. He swept one cold, disgusted look at Phoebe in a way that seemed to bracket her and the poet, and then moved away to talk with John Adam and Mr Cooper.

Finally, desperate, despite the fact they were surrounded by the Cooper family, the curate and the land agent, Robin and the lawyer, and Miss Belmont and the poet, she whispered to Felix to step to one side for a moment so that she could speak to him. As she'd hoped, his impeccable manners made him join her with no protest, but when he glanced at her, his face was hard and disdainful. He didn't look at her eyes; his gaze went coldly over her shoulder.

'Yes? What do you want?'

The coldness of his tone dried her throat and paralysed her mind. Phoebe struggled for the right thing to say, but no words came, only a great rush of emotion. She felt more and more upset that Felix was being so difficult . . . yet he'd kissed her which surely meant something . . . that he was making it impossible for her to speak . . . that he was hurting her . . .

'Nothing,' she said, and she heard her own voice shaking.

The silence stretched on and on. Phoebe felt a lump growing in her throat. She glanced up at him. His green eyes were distant, and if there was a message in them, she couldn't read it.

'I was mistaken,' she whispered.

His bow was a model of icy correctness as he turned and left her.

Phoebe was in despair. She'd wanted to talk to Felix about the weather and failed at that simple task. How ever could she instigate a complex conversation that would make him understand that she had never encouraged the poet to dangle after her, and that it would take a blunt instrument applied to the back of his head to stop him chasing after her with his dreadful verses?

The cold atmosphere between Phoebe and Felix grew thicker over the next few days, until a shimmering crystal screen seemed to separate them. The more Phoebe's heart ached, the more she refused to look at him. But, busy as she kept herself during the day, there was always the night to torment her. Sometimes she woke, flushed and disturbed by the memory of his kiss. She wished she had a mother to talk to — she couldn't tell Georgiana how her son was making her feel! Nor could she ask the dowager countess if Felix was acting out of character, not without telling her what they had quarrelled about, and how could she do that when Phoebe wasn't sure of the exact problem herself.

She didn't know what to think about his kiss, either. For sure he had been wrong to kiss her a second time, yet he'd promised, 'You have my heart'.

That she would never forget, and a thrill ran over her each time she remembered that passionate vow. Yet she worried that those whispered words had only been her imagination. Her brain told her to be sensible; her instincts told her to believe in what she had heard.

Confusion swirled in her heart. It was an effort to keep her demeanour tranquil, and even more of an effort to maintain a composed face while she and Felix held chilly conversations about the fate of porcelain vases and paintings of horses and one day the effort was too much. Her reserve cracked and she flew at him.

They were alone in the hall. Felix was examining gold coins that might have been Roman.

'This is a treasure hoard indeed. It's astonishing to think how long it has been lying forgotten in the attic.'

His expression was so serious as he weighed the gold in his palm. She felt sad, wistful, and unhappy about the gulf that had opened between them. What were they quarrelling about? Her heart caught and then sped on. She had to try again. Forget talking about the weather, she wanted the truth about their relationship.

'Felix, you are breaking my heart.'

His green eyes opened wide in surprise.

Phoebe's knees were shaking, but she persisted.

'What have I done? Why have you gone all closed on me?'

He lifted an eyebrow and gave her a look of masculine surprise. The cold distance in his eyes made a lump blossom in her throat. Tears sprang to her eyes and starred her vision. Of an instant her decision was made. She would leave. Strange how unappealing the notion of a little cottage with a piano now seemed, but she could not bear his coldness.

'I shall be looking to move very soon. I shall go next week if I can arrange it. Maybe I'll try Bath.'

His face crumpled. He masked his expression after one split second, but she saw agony there, and his words were pleading.

'Please don't go.'

'Felix, I don't understand you. Why do you want me to stay? You are ignoring me, aren't you?'

He didn't attempt to deny it.

'It's for the best. Believe me. It's for your own protection.'

'You're killing me,' she insisted, and then paused, at a loss for words, unable to understand this puzzling man.

Felix felt his heart pounding as he looked into Phoebe's lovely grey eyes. He could not bear her to leave. Colour and sunshine had come back into his life with Phoebe. He knew that the clouds of grey depression that had ruined his life before he met her would return if she left him. He felt as if he was cracking inside. The fog would return if she left him, he had no doubt of that. The idea of her leaving Elwood was a shock to him, but, now that she'd forced the idea onto his attention, it made sense that she would want to leave. He'd been so busy controlling his own feelings that he'd not stopped to consider hers. Now he looked into her eyes and examined her carefully.

Her love for him was written all over her face. Suddenly he was glad that she'd ignored all the 'off-limits' signals he'd been putting out and confronted him directly. Why wasn't he surprised that she would have the courage to tackle him head on? She was brave and strong and sparking and warm, or she had been when he met her. Now that he looked at her properly, he was shocked to see how thin she'd grown. Where had the strong and capable Phoebe gone? She looked like a vulnerable little girl, and he suddenly realised that the hollows under her cheekbones and the pansy-coloured shadows under her eyes had been put there by him, by his behaviour.

He was going to have to talk to her, to try to explain. Why had he been so blind? It had never occurred to him to wonder what interpretation she would put on his withdrawal. 'What have I done?' she'd asked him. She thought she was at fault. It wasn't fair to carry on letting her believe that she was the one in the wrong.

'All right,' he capitulated. 'I'll try to explain.'

And then he stopped because he didn't have the words to tell her what he needed to say, although the prospect of sharing his loneliness was strangely enticing.

'Let me think a minute,' he ordered.

And bless her, she did.

He had to be careful, and he had no experience in baring his soul. He was used to keeping himself aloof so it was hard to speak clearly of what was in his heart, but he owed it to her.

'I can never marry,' he told her. 'More, it is dangerous for me to have a relationship with a woman.'

Especially with a woman who can spark desire the way that you do, he thought, his eyes resting on Phoebe's gently curving lips.

'Can you tell me why?'

Her voice was gentle and coaxing, but he felt too ashamed of his bad blood to speak of it, not to this sweet and pure child.

'I cannot tell you exactly.'

Her raspberry-pink lips opened to speak and one of his hands flew up to motion her to silence.

'Please, ask me no more!'

But at the same time she said: 'Is it because of your father?'

Hearing it spoken aloud made him flinch, yet he owed her the truth, and there was relief too, in being understood.

'Yes.'

'I'm sorry. I can see this is painful for you, but I do want to understand you.' Her smile was warm and comforting. 'I know that British gentlemen do not like speaking about themselves! I'm glad you told me your secret, but I can't understand what you are worrying about. You are not in the least like your father.'

He was more like his father than she would ever know. At this very moment he was mad with the desire to pull her to him and wrap his arms around her sweet form. It would be such heaven to sink into her warmth.

Concentrate, he ordered himself.

'I could become like him if I allowed myself to do so. Blood runs deep and I have his passions.'

She touched his hand gently.

'Are you sure?'

'When I look at you, I am sure,' he admitted.

Phoebe shook her head.

'You would never hurt me.'

His heart swelled with love as he looked at her, but that was why he must keep to his resolve.

'You say that now, but who knows what the years might bring. What if we had a fight? I've seen it over and over again. Traits lie buried and surface under pressure. I cannot risk getting involved with a woman who makes me feel so passionate: there might be an explosion.'

He tensed, waiting for tears, anger, or a scene. He did not know what to expect. Phoebe looked at him with the world in her eyes.

'Then we must eliminate passion.'

'What do you mean?' he asked, but already some of the tension and misery of the last few weeks was washing away. He trusted Phoebe to have a plan, to save the situation as she so often had before.

'Come, we can be friends, can we not?' she was saying now. 'You do not wish to marry, very well. There must be no more kisses.' The look she threw at him was enchanting, and he could see in her eyes that she was remembering. 'There must be no more kisses,' she repeated. 'But, we can be friends; indeed, we must be friends, for I cannot bear to be estranged from you.'

There was funniness about her smile that he couldn't resist. He was so tired of being alone, of denying himself his heart's desire, and he knew now that she would make it easy for him. She knew he would not marry her. She would help him keep his passion in check. She would not tease him for more than he could give. Where would the harm be if they were friends?

'Come to the orphanage with me tomorrow,' she was urging now. 'The children would love to meet you.'

'I don't know what I'd say to them,' he protested.

He drove himself from dawn to dusk to take care of the estate, but he didn't know any of the tenants at all. His father couldn't have cared less about them, and his mother's health did not allow her to visit the poor. He had no idea how to behave.

'It'll be easy, you'll see. They are rehearsing the Christmas play. You can watch, and you must tell them how well they are doing, and everyone will be happy.'

He wasn't used to other people

telling him what he must do, but to his surprise he found himself almost willing to fall in with her plans.

'I should really be supervising the barley harvest,' he protested.

Phoebe cocked her head and examined his face.

'We can ride to the orphanage and back past the grain fields,' she told him. 'You do not need to be there all day. The men know their work.'

Perhaps that was true, this year. When Felix first returned the farm labourers had been very slack, but he'd bought them new equipment and trained them up so they should be able to manage without him. In fact, he knew they could. So why was he so reluctant to agree? He bit his lip and knew it was because he never let go and didn't know how to. The very idea was terrifying.

Phoebe's eyes were very bright.

'Is the notion of time off and a little relaxation so very frightening?'

He scowled at her before he could

stop himself. He always hid his feelings and nobody ever knew what he was thinking. The fact that she could see through his mask was alarming.

'There is no room in my life for relaxation,' he replied, a little stiffly.

'There is now,' she insisted, grinning.

He enjoyed sparring with her. He loved the fact that she wasn't afraid of him. Her view on life was so different from his own, and it intrigued him. Deep within him, steel chains let go. Perhaps the fields would be successfully harvested without him, and even if the operation wasn't perfect, he found that he didn't much care. Elwood didn't seem as important as usual, and it was a relief, but it was also a warning sign; deep within him alarm bells rang.

'Come, cousin,' Phoebe was saying now, 'you work harder than anyone on the whole estate and allow yourself no pleasure. A day out will do you good, and,' her eyes sparkled as she produced her clinching argument, 'it is your duty to supervise the welfare of the waifs of the parish.'

'Very well,' he acknowledged.

He could not resist her. Her friendly sweetness could heal him from the inside out. He could no longer bear to live in chilly isolation when such perfect companionship was being offered. Yet he was not wholly relaxed. Phoebe had charmed away the barriers that had protected him for so long, but he couldn't help asking himself if it was safe to live without them.

14

They rode out on a gorgeous autumn day. A fabulous harvest sun shone down on the wagons and the horses and the stacks of golden sheaves. All the time Felix was assuring the farm workers that they were doing a splendid job, which they were, his head was warning him that a day out with Phoebe wasn't a good idea. He tried to count the golden barley sheaves and couldn't. His concentration was shot to pieces and it was all her fault. He looked across at her and scowled.

The smile she sent back in return was full of sparkles and sunshine. She warmed his heart and it told him that going out with her was the best plan he'd had in years. Yet still the fear of losing control was deep in him. Change was a scary business.

'Don't look so beautiful! You promised that you'd help me to stay in control,' he reminded Phoebe.

She didn't seem worried by his sudden fierce comment.

'You'll be safe enough at the orphanage,' she replied with a merry smile. 'We will be surrounded by thirty little chaperones.'

What on earth would he say to all those children?

Phoebe laughed at his gloomy face.

'You'll enjoy yourself,' she prophesised.

'Plays by children are not my thing.'

'How do you know? Have you seen one before?'

'No,' he admitted.

'It will be fun.'

He couldn't help pulling a face. He'd never had the slightest interest in children, nor any desire to breed. His Arab horses were enough for him. He couldn't see the appeal in raising a family.

'I don't know how I let you talk me into this.'

'Come, It's a gorgeous day — I want us to enjoy it and not waste time arguing.'

He turned his horse obediently towards the orphanage, but he had to ask: 'Haven't you had enough orphans in your life that you have to adopt thirty more?'

'I haven't adopted them, but until we find the right person to run the orphanage, they need me.'

Duty was a simple instinct with her, he mused as they rode side by side in the sunlight. He respected her because she understood that duty must come first. Perhaps he was safe with Phoebe because she understood why he felt that he must keep away from her. It eased a pain in him to know that she knew the truth about him and accepted it.

The children had been watching for them. They tumbled out into the yard screaming with delight. Felix watched Phoebe hugging the children and greeting the vicar. How beautifully she dealt with people. She was friendly and charming, yet she was firm. The children adored her, but they respected her too. She looked at home running the orphanage. She knew how to manage to perfection. She would make a wonderful countess. She was kneeling now with a child in each arm and Felix's heart melted. She'd make a wonderful mother. And of a sudden the urge to have a family gripped him by the throat. He knew with every fibre of his being that they would have beautiful children together. His son would make a fabulous job of running Elwood and the estate.

A primitive possessiveness flared up in him. For the first time, he realised that he didn't want his cousin's family taking over the estate. The man was a selfish prig and his children were spoilt. They'd treat the land like a moneybox for their own benefit. His conscience jabbed him. Wasn't he failing in his duty to his home if he passed on the mantle to people who would not take care of it? Surely it would be better for his own children to inherit Elwood.

The picture was enticing, but then he remembered how he'd sworn never to risk handing on his parent's bad character. Look what happened! He'd taken one step and allowed a little ease and friendship into his life, the next he was longing to marry Phoebe and have children with her, and that was frightening. He should never have broken his code of behaviour for her. He had to escape.

'I have changed my mind. I cannot allow the grain harvest to proceed without my supervision.'

Phoebe simply laughed at him.

'Watch the play. It will be more fun than you think.'

He was still wary of emotional involvement, but it was hard to resist the appeal in her eyes and the children were flocking around him, tugging at his fingers and showing him to his chair. There was no escape!

As Felix settled his handsome figure in front of the makeshift stage Phoebe couldn't help being thrilled to discover that she could make him act out of character. Now that she'd persuaded him to stay, she would have to make sure that he enjoyed himself!

'Act one,' she called.

Mary and Joseph took up residence in the stable. Three very stout angels giggled as they announced that a child was born. The shepherds watched their sheep, and the three wise kings clomped across the stage bearing gifts. Felix could now say with complete honesty that children's plays were not his thing. Phoebe assured him that the children were still rehearsing and the nativity scenes would be a triumph on the night, but he suspected that no matter how well the play were done, he would be still able to take it or leave it, but the joy and exuberance on Phoebe's face as she marshalled her charges was a memory he'd treasure forever.

The vicar walked over to him, smiling, bowing and rubbing his hands.

'When am I to have the pleasure of

calling the banns?' he enquired, archly.

Felix turned and raised one eyebrow.

'I'm very sorry, my lord. I didn't mean to presume, but from the way you are looking at Miss Allen I was sure that I heard wedding bells.'

'How do I look at her?'

'You look at her with love in your eyes.'

Did he really look at her like that? Then he'd better stop looking.

'We are not marrying,' he replied shortly.

Realising he'd dropped a clanger, the vicar scurried away.

Felix went back to watching Phoebe. She shone in this setting — as she did in every setting. No wonder people thought they would marry. She would look so right, by his side, running the estate. Beautiful as she was, he wasn't feeling desire at this moment but a sweeter, deeper feeling. He knew that Phoebe would be a good friend to him, a support by his side in every circumstance, his friend on all occasions. Yet there was a primitive element to his feelings as well. He could imagine her — radiant with a new-born baby. He'd love to see her with his son and heir, or his daughter and his delight. The longing that bloomed in his heart horrified him. He had to deny himself these tender feelings, didn't he? They could only lead to disaster.

Raised voices drew his attention back to the room. The play was over, the children has rushed away to change, and his darling was confronting the vicar in the empty room. He couldn't help smiling at the outrage on Phoebe's face.

'A few toys at Christmas will not spoil these children.'

The vicar saw that Felix was attending and bowed his way.

'His lordship is already most generous, and we must remember that foundlings do not have the same expectations as do children who are more happily circumstanced.'

'All the more reason to give them a

treat,' Phoebe insisted. She turned to Felix. Mischief sparkled in her eyes, and he felt that she made the world around her light up.

'Look at this carved toy! The workmanship is fantastic. The vicar says it was made by a local woodcarver.'

She dropped a little wooden carving into his hands, still warm from the contact with her fingers. It was a robin, whittled with life and vigour. Its cheeky expression reminded Felix of Phoebe.

'It's a remarkable likeness. Who made it?'

The vicar replied, 'Peter Shackleton. He lives on top of the moors.'

'Oh, I know the chap you mean. He lives by the forest and makes chairs, doesn't he? I didn't know he did such good carvings as well.'

'His toys are much in demand at Christmas.'

'And the demand has just increased by thirty,' Phoebe said.

'I'm sure his lordship won't approve of spoiling these children. We mustn't make them soft. Don't forget, they will have to work hard and make their way in life when they leave the orphanage.'

Phoebe's expressive grey eyes turned towards Felix. He knew her so well. She didn't wish to embarrass the vicar by contradicting him. He was a good man and did a lot for the children in his own way, but she didn't have to say aloud that she was determined that the children should have presents for Christmas, it was written all over her face!

Felix smiled gently at the vicar.

'If Miss Allen wishes the children to have toys, then you had best send word to the toymaker at once. You must of course send the bill to me for this Christmas order.'

Then he laughed at himself for being so easily manipulated. All it had taken was one look, but he felt good about it. Phoebe was right. What was wrong with making people happy?

The vicar stopped arguing.

'I shall send word tomorrow. Shackleton lives right on top of the moors and it's a good long hike up the fell to his cottage.'

'Thank you,' Phoebe said, giving him a sunny smile.

Then she turned to Felix and really smiled as their eyes met and he realised just how radiant her smile could be. She touched his hand with the lightest butterfly brush.

'Thank you,' she breathed quietly.

The children came tumbling back into the room, washed and changed and ready for high tea, but it was as if they were alone. Even in such a crowd, Felix felt as if they were alone together as he and Phoebe sat at the long tea table, until that is, a small stout child ended up in his lap.

'Who is this?' he protested.

'Little Jems needs help with his milk,' Phoebe told him.

He would have thrust the toddler back at her, but she already had a child on each knee, so once more he submitted to her will. Little Jems was a warm cosy armful. He ate sugar biscuits with brio and drank his milk like a gentleman. Felix found the whole process of giving a child its tea unexpectedly satisfying and even gave him a cuddle.

'You are sweet,' Phoebe told him.

'I can be nice sometimes,' Felix told her.

But he knew that he was reacting to her tutoring. She was teaching him that you didn't have to listen to your head all the time, that it was okay to relax and to have fun.

Phoebe smiled with stars in her eyes. She was clearly thrilled to see him happy. Perhaps because of that, as they rode towards the barley fields on the way home, he admitted to her, 'This has been a fun day.'

It was lovely to see her glow with the knowledge that she'd given him something special. And it had been a special day. He hadn't expected her idea of a good time to work for him, but playing with the children had been magical.

When they got to the barley fields the harvest was proceeding at a good rate. Felix didn't have a single fault to find. No catastrophe had occurred because he'd been away for the day on a jaunt. Maybe it was okay to have fun every now and then. Phoebe had been right again.

He turned his head to look at her small figure riding so valiantly next to him. He almost admitted that he loved her, an impulse that shocked him to the core. He cared deeply and completely, he knew that now, but it wasn't a good idea to say it, even though she knew that he had sworn never to marry. It might make her want more than he could give.

But the smile she shot back at him was uncomplicated and friendly and he remembered that he could trust her. Her friendship was all he needed.

And he barely even noticed what he'd admitted. Only a week ago he would have corrected himself mentally and said that he didn't need anyone.

15

A week later, word arrived at Elwood (via the Boot's sister, whose brother worked for the coaching inn) that Robin would be arriving at three o'clock that day.

At three o'clock, Felix and Phoebe made their way to the gravel sweep at the front of the house and stood a few feet apart in comfortable silence, waiting, along with all the household including the Coopers, to welcome Robin. Phoebe sneaked a glance at Felix. The wind was playing havoc with his hair. The softer look suited him.

Pepe gave a yip, and Phoebe came out of her thoughts and became aware of galloping hooves.

Felix frowned as a small figure on a horse crested the hill and galloped pell-mell towards them.

'That can't be Robin! He'd never use a horse so.'

Now they saw a tiny splodge of puce livery. It was a servant that Phoebe didn't recognise. The man was plying his whip vigorously, and his chestnut horse was covered in sweat. The poor beast's eyes rolled wildly as it slid to a halt in a slither of gravel and flying foam.

Felix's dark eyebrows frowned in disproval as he inspected the hysterically shaking animal.

'What message is urgent enough to ruin a horse for?' he growled.

'Sir, it's urgent, sir,' gasped the servant. 'My master, Mr Butcher, sent me to inform you that the horse you sold him has turned wild and had to be destroyed, sir.'

The servant shifted his weight from foot to foot.

'Sir, the beast went berserk and attacked one of the grooms. It trampled him badly, and then it went for my master so he took up his gun and shot it.'

Phoebe felt ice water cascade down her spine.

'Not one of Shaitan's foals,' she gasped.

She looked up at Felix and from the expression on his face she saw that this news was the last thing that Felix was expecting. For the first time ever she saw him looking surprised and off balance.

'Impossible!'

'Sir, I'm afraid so, sir.'

Felix's voice was low and shocked.

'Tell your master I shall wait upon him at once.'

The intensity in his tone made Phoebe think that he was suffering deeply, and when she saw the agony in his eyes her heart felt as if it were bleeding.

'You had better leave your mount and take a horse from my stable, but don't you dare treat it ill. Understand? Ride slowly on the way home.'

'Sir! Yes, sir!'

Felix stared after the departing puce

back of the servant. His face was ice and stone and bitter despair.

'I've been a complete fool. What was I thinking to let down my guard? Blood always tells.'

Phoebe could see that he was speaking to himself, but the emotion that roughened his voice tore at her heart. Suddenly the true import of the news hit her.

'Felix, you can't let this terrible tragedy affect you.'

His eyes were dark with pain as he turned to her.

'It proves my point. Blood always tells. Shaitan's foals may appear all right on the surface, but there is a bad streak in them. You cannot trust them. You never know when they will turn vicious and hurt somebody.'

She could see shutters closing off his heart, taking him away from her.

Mr Cooper, who had been standing close to them and openly listening, stepped forward.

'Now then, Chando, think on: what

may be true of horses isn't true of men, not real men like you.'

But the familiar frost was clouding Felix's eyes, chilling the atmosphere. The bow he gave Mr Cooper was so chilly that the tradesman clicked his tongue and moved away. The bow he made to Phoebe was very little warmer.

'Pray excuse me. I must wait upon Mr Butcher at once.'

Her knees began to tremble beneath her, but she ran after him.

'I'll come with you.'

He swung around and snarled at her in the voice of a stranger.

'Don't you see that this incident proves we should never be together?'

Looking pale and grave, Felix strode away, his boot heels clicking firmly on the marble floor. Phoebe ran no further after him. Her heart warned her that he was determined to close her out; besides, another horse was approaching so she had to turn back and stand with the group of household members on the great stone terrace at Elwood, watching Robin arrive. A soft wind blew, fluttering the maid's aprons. The white handkerchief Robin was waving whipped like a flag in his hand.

'Hello! What news?' he called as he dismounted from his horse.

Tears stung Phoebe's eyes.

'Oh, Robin, it's not good . . . ' she told him, and poured out the tale.

'Wait until we've heard the whole story,' he advised her.

But Felix's expression was even grimmer when he returned from visiting the neighbour. She wanted to ask for more details, but his manner made it plain that he was not going to speak with her. He sat by Mr Cooper at dinner and the two men spoke very little. In contrast, Phoebe couldn't help but notice that Alicia was chatting more than she ever had. She was plainly delighted to have Robin back.

After dinner, Phoebe waited by the door of the library, but when the men joined the ladies, Felix brushed past her in such a forceful way that she dared not follow him to stand by one of the long windows. She stood helplessly as Robin went to join him. She knew that the two men hadn't had the chance to exchange news yet, so she chose to sit in a chair as close to the two men as feasible and frankly listened. Robin straight away asked what she wanted to know: 'Is it true that the horse went berserk?'

The curate walked between them and Phoebe lost a few words. She leaned as close to the two men as she possibly could without falling over. She could hear Felix speaking sadly.

'I've a good mind to shoot Shaitan . . . '

The rest of his words were drowned by the poet.

'I say, Phoebe, I've written a new poem.'

'Go away!' she cried.

'But it's dedicated to you,' he bleated.

Gordon-Rose settled on a low stool at her feet, unfolded his poem with a great deal of unnecessary paper crackling, and began declaiming in his special poetry voice.

'Beauty walks o'er the sky like the sun.

'But the sun in my life is Phoebe . . . '

Phoebe cursed the code of manners that prevented her from getting up from her seat and openly listening to Felix and Robin. She watched their faces and tried to lip read, but she couldn't pick up a word. Felix's expression was adamant; Robin seemed to be protesting.

Miss Belmont scurried over, butting in between Phoebe and her nephew.

'Gordon, Gordon, the curate wishes to speak to you.'

'But I'm reading my poetry.'

'Go on,' Phoebe said, giving the startled poet a good push. 'Do as your aunt says.'

But it was too late to hear any more. Robin patted Felix's shoulder, but then he went to sit by Alicia. His head was close to hers and they were both talking hard, and happily. Phoebe could hear frequent laughter. Felix remained standing by the tall window, a shadow falling across his face. He kissed his mother and left the library soon afterwards, leaving Phoebe to worriedly mull over the situation.

Phoebe watched him anxiously over the next week, but Felix made no move to shoot his stallion. It didn't reassure her. His manner made it plain that he had decided to cut her out of his life. He didn't speak to her or look at her. She thought once more of moving to Bath, to the peace of a little cottage and her piano, but the idea held less appeal than ever. In fact it felt like running away, because now she knew why he was shutting her out. He might not trust himself but she knew he was a good man. She knew that they could be happy together if only he would believe in himself. She wasn't going to run away. She was going to convince him to give them and their love a chance, but she also knew that she would have to give him time and space to get over the setback.

To control her worry and heartbreak, she threw herself into the task of supervising the cleaning and packing of the attic contents, and it proceeded twice as fast as before. But underneath the business of organising the clearing and packing of treasures, of supervising the kitchens, and accompanying Georgiana to the garden as the days ticked past, there was the terrible fear that maybe she couldn't break down his barriers, and that Felix had shut her out of his life forever.

16

In the middle of December, Mr Cooper announced that Robin and Alicia were engaged to be married.

'Mrs Cooper wasn't happy about him being the youngest son,' he confided in Phoebe. 'She'd set her heart on an earl she had, but anyone can see it's a love match between them and the family is an old one. Did you know they came over with Charlemagne?'

'Really?' murmured Phoebe.

'And after all, I said to her, well, Mother, at least you'll be able to talk about your daughter Lady Hathaway and she gradually became reconciled. And it could be a good thing that he has no land of his own to speak of. I'm not fond of these crumbling piles. 'Pick a spot and I'll build you a new house as a wedding present,' I told them.'

'Where will they live?'

Mr Cooper's face split in a generous smile.

'Blow me if they haven't taken a fancy to settling somewhere near Elwood. You'll be neighbours.'

The Coopers began to pack up, saying that they needed to visit Robin's family and buy wedding clothes in London, but then Elwood was rocked by the news that the Prince of Wales was coming to stay for a night so that he could hunt with the local hounds and the Coopers quickly unpacked again. Mrs Cooper was quivering with excitement at the thought of meeting royalty.

The prince had given them very short notice, and it was true that they only had twenty-four hours to get ready for the royal visit, but somehow they had all managed to overlook the piles of half-packed antiques spread across the tiled floor of the great hall until the moment the youngest page boy ran in to say that the prince and his party were at the gatehouse.

Felix rode out on his horse to meet the royal guests and escort them to the house, but as the household assembled to greet them, Georgiana let out a shriek.

'Why has nobody cleared the hall? It's like an obstacle course!'

Phoebe gazed in horror at an assortment of items that included a Welsh harp, a shield that had been at the battle of Hastings, three ottomans and a chaise longue. One couldn't expect the prince regent to hop over a sideboard in order to reach the dining room.

'Don't you worry, Miss Allen,' O'Neil cried. 'We'll have this junk shifted in a jiffy. Come on you lot! All of you! Yes, even you, Miss Belmont! You can carry a diddy little candelabrum, can't you?'

The major domo whipped the staff into such effective action that everyone was lined up and looking innocent as the carriages arrived, and Felix stepped into a hall that was nearly empty. It is true that Peter galloped past him dragging a stuffed bear, followed by O'Neil hugging a suit of armour, but the coast was clear as the royal personage entered.

Of course Felix had spotted the scurrying footmen. Phoebe looked at him anxiously, and was delighted when his left eyelid flickered ever so slightly. It was the first time he'd acknowledged her existence in weeks, but there was no chance to speak to him with such a swirl of august visitors demanding attention.

She couldn't help hoping that his friendly wink meant that he was thawing. The idea sent thrills all around her body and stained her cheeks red. She could only pray that if anyone noticed her discomposure, they'd think that she was all of a flutter over meeting the prince. The prince regent was as charming as all the reports made him out to be, but Phoebe didn't want to converse with a prince: she wanted Felix!

The rest of the party wanted lunch,

and she'd hardly been introduced to the last of them when the first of the party had freshened up and were back in the hall and they all had to go into the dining room.

Phoebe couldn't believe how formal and dressed up everyone was for a simple lunch in the country. The prince's friends were so glamorous that Phoebe forgave Jenny for having made her start to get ready at dawn that morning. Kitty had filled a copper bath with hot water and soap that smelt of lemons, and what a mixed pleasure it had been, to feel the hot water cascading over her skin, the clouds of bubbles sliding down her shoulders, and to feel the tremor in her belly that said today was maybe the day that she made it up with Felix.

Despite the December cold, it was a beautifully sunny day, and golden rays poured in thorough the spotless glass of the long windows. Sunlight sparkled on the silver, glittered on the jewellery of the women and reflected from the decorations that the men wore.

Thank goodness Miss Michaels had sent over a fashionable dress of violet with a lilac overdress of crepe. Thank goodness Jenny had insisted that she wear the new gown that morning, and most of all, Phoebe thought, thank goodness that Jenny had taught Kitty how to work magic with hair. She reached up and touched one of the white flowers that starred her dark curls. Her fingers shook, and she put them back in her lap.

Phoebe's pulse raced as she scanned the table. Robin was sitting next to her and the prince was on her other side but Felix was three seats away. As she watched his dark head, the sights and sounds of the dining table seemed to fade away. He looked up. Their eyes met. He was looking at her properly again. It was like a miracle. Her mouth dried. Her heart beat fast, fast, fast. His green eyes shone like burnished emeralds. A fire burned in the heart of the irises that spoke to her soul.

'Rather jolly, that tower of ice thing,' boomed a voice in her ear.

One couldn't be rude. She tore her gaze away from Felix and turned her attention to the royal personage and the table. She saw that Adolphe had sent in lobsters, jellies, soup, and the tower of ice cream that had so enthused the prince. The prince regent was plying his silver spoon with gusto, and his plump round cheeks were pink with delight.

She smiled dutifully up at the royal personage and made a light-hearted remark, which must have made some kind of sense because the prince laughed. He was charming and he seemed determined to be nice to her, but Phoebe would have given anything for ten minutes alone with Felix.

It was the same story when they went out on the horses. She couldn't get near Felix. Word of the royal visitor had spread and everyone in the area was out for the hunt, which was already popular because it was said to be one of the best in England. The countryside was looking its best and the hounds ran beautifully so everybody was happy, everybody but Phoebe. She was watching Felix, wishing she could be alone with him, and so she noticed when he turned away from the main hunt and into a lane bordered by ash trees. She swung away from the hunt and galloped under the silvery arch of bare branches. Then she heard angry shouting in a furious male voice. She got a cold feeling at the base of her spine. A stocky man in a red coat was plying a vicious black whip across the shivering hide of his horse.

'Stop! Oh, pray stop hitting your horse,' she called.

Felix had reined in his mount, experiencing the hesitation that any gentleman would feel before interfering in another's affairs, but he felt totally involved when the stocky man turned at Phoebe's shout and he saw the ugly look on the man's face. A look he'd seen on his father's face, before he lost control and thrashed a young horse or threw a sum that would pay a year's bills onto the card table. He'd spent years watching his father ruin things, because he was too young and too small to stop him, but this time he could act.

But before he could move, a small tornado rushed past him.

'Stop hitting your horse,' Phoebe cried again.

The man did stop, but only to curl his lip and swear at her, finishing his tirade with an ugly shout.

'It's none of your business how I treat my horse. It's a slug and it ruined my day out by making a fool of me in front of royalty.'

Now Felix felt anger racing through him, but he made a conscious effort to hold it in check, to meet violence with calm, not more violence.

'You may feel that the right to mistreat your horse is a private matter, but the way you talk to my cousin is, however, very much my business and I cannot allow you to speak to her so.'

He might have known that Phoebe

would be unmoved by the man's revolting diatribe, nor was she to be deflected from the matter at hand. She planted both hands on her hips and glared at the man.

'That mare is far too light and delicate for you.'

'I'll send it for horsemeat,' the man groused.

'You need a horse that can carry your weight,' Phoebe told him, and she turned to Felix with a world of trust in her eyes.

'Could we not find a more suitable mount for this man? Perhaps you could swap horses with him.'

But the man let out a bellow of rage.

'Are you trying to kill me? Don't you know that Chando is riding one of Shaitan's spawn? I swore that I'd never go near a horse with that bloodline again, and I mean it. They should all be shot the way that I shot mine.'

For a moment Felix was distracted from the problem before him. Phoebe's face was a study as she realised that this man must be the Mr Butcher whose horse had gone berserk. There was a little furrow between her brows as she thought furiously, and he couldn't help but wonder what she'd say next. He had come to admire her ideas and her problem-solving ability. Her consideration for revolting Mr Butcher had initially astonished him, but she was right. What good would it do to give the man a taste of his own medicine, which had been his own first thought? Phoebe's approach was better. If they found the man a horse that was up to his weight, then all would be well.

The thunder of hooves announced John Adam, followed by a bouncing Mr Cooper. The urban tradesman had never hunted before his visit to Elwood, so Spiller had mounted him on a sturdy cob, but everyone had remarked upon Mr Cooper's light hands and sensitivity to his horse's feelings. Felix felt a surge of pleasure as he realised the answer was before him. It took only a few seconds to swap the horses around to everybody's satisfaction. Mr Butcher galloped off to follow the hunt and the glamorous royal visitor who was the real attraction. The land agent and the tradesman followed hard at his heels. He should follow them, but Phoebe called to him to wait a moment, and he could not bear to leave her.

She rode her pony close to him and leaned out of the saddle to stroke the nose of his horse.

'Be careful,' Felix warned.

'Kamil is gentle as a kitten, but that is because you use him kindly. I am convinced in my own mind that Mr Butcher's horse went berserk because the man is so cruel and heavy-handed.'

Could she be right? There were some who said that harsh treatment could ruin a horse's temperament. Was it bad blood or cruelty that had sent the horse wild? Felix's head and his heart were ripping him apart. He wanted to believe her, but the very strength of his feelings for her were proof that he could be swayed by passion, that he might end up becoming the type of man he hated most in the world.

'Please don't put yourself at risk,' he said shortly. 'You know Kamil has bad blood in him. I would never trust him with a lady.'

Phoebe's heart ached for the pain she could see in his eyes. He was talking about himself as much as about his horse.

'Was Shaitan ever mistreated?' she asked.

'I don't know. I could make enquires, but please, do keep away from Kamil's teeth. He may bite you.'

Felix looked so anxious that she removed her hand and stopped petting his horse, although she was convinced there was no danger. Her heart ached for him and all that he had never had. She had been sad when she lost her father, but what a fine example he'd set her while he had been alive. He had shown so much love to his child and taught her so much about how to live. Poor Felix had never been able to admire his father, or to follow his example. A rush of anger shook her. Surely the worst thing the old earl had done was to make Felix believe evil of himself? She was shocked to discover that he could entertain even for a moment the notion that he had bad blood or could ever act wrongly.

'Felix, please listen to me. When have you ever, ever acted like your father?'

His green eyes flickered.

'I keep myself in check.'

'You have wonderful self-control. If you did not get angry with that horrible man, surely you can trust yourself to act correctly in any situation. You are not a selfish man. You always do your duty. You are kind to your horses, you take care of your tenants, and you were so wonderful with the children. Can you not believe me when I say that I would trust you with my life?'

'It is not safe to think that way.'

'We could be so good together,' she said, softly and sadly. 'Keep on believing in bad blood, and your father will ruin our future as well as your past.'

'He is dead. He can do no further damage.'

'Your eyes are flickering. You are lying to me. I think you know that your father is keeping us apart when we belong together.'

'I can't take the risk.'

'I trust you. Look how you handled Mr Butcher. You didn't use violence or even bad language.'

Felix could feel emotion welling up in him. He wanted to listen to her, to believe in her, because if what she was saying was true, then he was free to take her in his arms and kiss her until they were both dizzy and then marry her right there on the spot. He'd never wanted anything so much in his life before. Any second now his control would snap . . . any second . . .

Phoebe's grey eyes were brimming with tears.

'Felix, you don't take after your father at all. You have your mother's eyes; you have your own personality. Tell me — in what way are you like your father?'

Goaded beyond endurance, he shouted at her.

'In the violence of my feelings for you, can you not see that I am wild about you?'

There was no fear in her eyes.

'But you are controlling yourself. You are nothing like him. I cannot understand why you are torturing yourself with an idea that was surely formed when you were too young to fully understand the world.'

'I was old enough to feel my father hurting and humiliating both me and my mother. He never paused for even a flicker of a second before reaching out to take what he wanted. I have sworn that I will never be like him.'

'You are not. You are nothing like him.'

'I have his blood. I can't trust myself.'

'What reason do you have to think

that you would ever snap?'

Only the desperate pain in Phoebe's eyes forced the truth from him.

'You have never been on a battlefield if you have to ask a man that question. When my blood was hot, I found myself able to commit acts of violence that make me shudder. The men I killed haunt my dreams.'

'You were trained and ordered to do so. It was your duty. Have you killed or in any way injured a man since your return?'

'Well, no, but who knows what may happen in the future? Phoebe, can't you understand that by staying away, I am trying to protect you. I don't want to hurt you.'

'You are hurting me!'

He knew it was the truth. The pain in her eyes told him so. Oh, would he ever get away from his past? He was tormenting the one woman in the world whom he wished to make happy. He wanted to wrap his arms around her and protect her from all harm, but he couldn't protect her from himself. He hated himself.

'Felix — ' Phoebe began.

'Please. Please don't try me further.'

His voice sounded harsh in his ears, but that was because it was choked with the tears he wished he could shed. He gazed helplessly at his true love. Liquid stars glittered in Phoebe's eyes. She looked back at him for a long second and then she squared her shoulders, nodded and turned away.

Phoebe's heart was breaking, but she would not push him further, not after such a heartfelt plea.

'I'm so sorry, Felix,' she whispered.

He gave Kamil the signal to move forward. Her little pony trotted to keep up. She rode next to him in silence.

'Do you want to try to find the hunt?' Felix asked her.

'Let's go home. No, not home, to your house. Felix, I cannot bear this. I must leave Elwood.'

'You cannot leave before Christmas,' he said.

He knew he was being a fool. As usual she had faced the matter with her usual courage. If they could not be together then one of them must leave, and it couldn't be him. She was right, and yet he made no effort to curb the impulse to delay her departure. Quickly he found an excuse.

'You cannot disappoint the children. You must stay until Christmas.'

'True,' she replied in a flat voice. 'I will leave in the New Year.'

The horses were pleased to turn for their stables and moved briskly towards Elwood. Phoebe was slumped on her cream pony, and every detail of her posture showed that she was depressed. Felix was moved by Phoebe's misery and the knowledge that he had caused it. Could she be right? Was he making her unhappy over a figment of his imagination; a mistaken idea from his long-lost youth? Maybe it was time he made peace with the past, but until he was sure, it would be better if he didn't speak to her again.

He kept to his vow with a stony resolve that Phoebe found very hard to bear. He didn't look at her or speak to her and her heart felt as if it were turning to ice. The weather turned bitterly cold and frosty and the dark of an English winter added to the depression she was battling.

Two days before Christmas, she was trying to concentrate on the task of sorting and listing the contents of a casket of antique jewellery that had been unearthed in the attics, but the first bracelet she lifted was set with emeralds. The dull green fire reminded her of Felix's eyes. Pain clawed at her heart, followed by tears pushing up inside her. She'd tried so hard to be stoic and bear Felix's behaviour, but now the storm was upon her. She'd break out weeping any moment. She told the poet that she had a sick headache and would dine in her room.

Even in her room she couldn't cry in peace. Jenny and Kitty flew in to see what the matter with her was. She sent them away on the pretext that even the slightest noise made her head worse, and then, finally, she was able to collapse on her bed and give in to tears.

Pain had been stalking her heart for weeks now, but she'd been keeping it away by daily assuring herself that she would find a way to get through to Felix before Christmas and all would be well. But she'd been fooling herself. The deadline was upon her. There was no hope and the pain broke free to tear at her heart.

She lay on her beautiful bed, and her mind felt dazed and slow. The usually obedient Pepe refused to stay in his basket and insisted on lying next to her. Phoebe gave in and held his warm body close for comfort. He nuzzled her sweetly. He seemed to know she needed comfort.

Time passed unevenly: a second seemed to last a forever of stinging pain, then the light from the windows was fading and a whole day had slipped away.

Jenny came to check on her, but Phoebe pretended to be asleep and the woman tiptoed away. Phoebe lay quiet in the silent room, her eyes wide open, watching the gathering darkness drain the colour from the pink fabric ceiling of her four-poster bed.

Sleep was no refuge when it came. Her dreams were stalked by a dark-haired man who paced like a wolf, howling that he had bad blood and was dangerous. She wanted to cry out and tell him that he was mistaken, that she loved him and trusted him, but her voice was smothered by a cloud of mist. She half-woke, shivering with pain and cold. She rolled over in the vast bed and wrapped her arms around the sadness in her heart; and then she realised that she was physically cold and the light in the room was different.

Kitty tiptoed in noisily. Silver rattled on china as the maid banged a heavy wooden tray onto the table by the side of the bed.

'What time is it?' Phoebe asked sleepily.

'Miss, it's gone eight o'clock, miss. Is your headache better?'

What headache? She didn't get headaches. Then Phoebe remembered. Heavens, the lies she'd told yesterday! She hated to tell lies, but a headache was much more acceptable as an excuse than a broken heart. And, although she was weary and heartbroken, in an odd sort of way she felt as if a crisis was behind her. She had accepted her fate. She blessed her allowance because it meant that she could live an independent life, a single independent life, for she'd never forget Felix, but there were worse fates than being a spinster in a little cottage. She was able to smile at Kitty and speak with perfect truth.

'Yes, I'm feeling better, thank you.'

'We're all snowed up and it's still snowing. At least three feet fell in the night and there are deep snowdrifts on the moors. That's lovely for Christmas

Eve. I love a white Christmas, don't you?'

Phoebe sat bolt upright.

'Felix was to pick up the toys for the children today. I hope he can still ride up the moors to the toymaker's cottage. The children will be so disappointed if there is nothing in their stockings for Christmas.'

'Don't you worry! That wonderful horse of his won't take any notice of a bit of snow.'

But when Phoebe went down to breakfast, Felix was dressed in his house clothes. It was an effort to approach him, knowing that he didn't wish to speak to her, but today she must.

'Will the snow stop you riding up on the moors where the toymaker lives?'

His harsh expression lifted for a moment.

'I had not forgotten, but you know that the Duke of Preston is staying with us and I have promised to show him around the stables today. He is buying one of Shaitan's foals and plans to race it.'

'Will you be able to go for the toys later?'

'Possibly, depending what time the duke arrives downstairs. You know it goes dark early. If it's too late to set out, I will go tomorrow.'

'But it's Christmas tomorrow! I wanted the children to have their presents in the morning.'

'What's the difference if they get the presents the next day?'

Phoebe quite understood that Felix couldn't keep a duke waiting, especially one who she had been introduced to her as a near neighbour and a good friend of the family, but it was infuriating that he didn't understand the importance of Christmas Day. Well, if Felix was busy, she'd just have to go herself.

'There's a world of difference. Of course they must have their stockings. I'll go and get the presents.'

Felix laughed as he strolled out of the

room, saying as he left, 'Have you seen how deep the snow is? Your little pony's legs would never make it. Stop fussing. I will fetch your toys tomorrow if I cannot today.'

The lazy condescension in his tone flicked Phoebe on the raw. She ran to the window and rubbed a patch in the frost crystals. The garden was transformed under a heavy white layer of snow. It was deep. How annoying of Felix to be right. Her little horse would struggle to wade through those snowdrifts. She bit her lip. Her only comfort over the last few miserable weeks had been thinking of the children's happiness when they opened their presents on Christmas morning. She couldn't bear the disappointment. She wished she could take Kamil and go herself. His long legs would go through snow.

And then the idea came to her. If she took the horse and came to no harm, surely Felix would abandon his stiff-necked conviction that bad blood was inherited. She knew she was taking a risk. She was gambling her life that the horse wasn't vicious and would carry her safely, but she would rather die in the attempt than spend the rest of her life in a lonely cottage wishing she'd tried harder to get through to Felix. And besides, if she was right, where was the risk? Although she was almost sure that Kamil was safe, her heart was beating very fast as she ran up the stairs to her room.

'Kitty, please will you ask the duke's valet what time his master usually gets up.'

She was halfway into her blue riding habit by the time Kitty returned.

'The valet says the duke is a late riser. He's never opened his eyes this morning and he won't stir for another hour at least. Surely you're not riding in all this snow?'

'I thought I'd wear my habit because I am visiting the stables with the duke. Button me up, please, Kitty.'

More lies! Phoebe thought as Kitty

helped her into the habit, but it would never do to let Kitty know her plan.

She tiptoed out of the house and sneaked into the stable yard. The good smells of hay and horses hung in the crisp cold air. The paths and yard had already been swept clear of snow. She had no idea how she was going to get past Spiller, who would surely never allow her to take Kamil, so she stood in the cold under the clock arch surveying the scene until one of the stable lads scurried by.

'Good morning. Tommy Lane, isn't it?'

'Yes, my lady.'

'Where is Spiller?'

'He's in the back paddock catching the nag what the Duke of Preston wants to buy. Shall I fetch him for you?'

'No, no. You can help me. I want you to put a ladies' saddle on Kamil for me, please.'

The lad's eyes bugged wide.

'Hurry up,' Phoebe snapped.

Her tone was much sharper than she

would ever normally use, but she knew that if she gave the lad time to think he would start objecting, and Spiller could be back at any moment.

'I'm in a great hurry,' she added.

He was reluctant, you could see that from his puzzled face and slow movements, but he didn't dare oppose a direct order from her and so he fetched the right harness. Kamil snorted and looked pleased as they entered his stable. Phoebe stroked his black nose and then helped young Tommy with the leather straps and silver buckles.

'Quickly,' she urged him.

Although she didn't think Kamil had ever carried a lady before, he lined up with the mounting block as if he did it every day of the week and stood quietly while Phoebe got into the saddle.

'There's Spiller coming up the road,' cried little Tommy with clear relief. 'Wait a minute, my lady.'

But Phoebe was clattering out of the yard and urging Kamil into the white wilderness outside.

17

It was nearly midday by the time the Duke of Preston was ready to visit the horses and Felix was able to escort his distinguished guest to the stables. He was astonished to walk into not the usual calm good order of Spiller's domain, but a first-class row. His groom appeared to be thrashing a howling boy in the middle of the cobbles.

'Spiller!' he snapped.

He'd expected his head groom to be recalled to his duties by the presence of his master and his important guest, but the head groom showed no signs of returning to his normal calm manner. Instead he turned his wrathful face towards Felix and blurted out,

'I'm sorry, your lordship but I only just found out. Lane here, he was afraid to tell me because he knew he'd done wrong.'

'You always tells me to do what the quality says,' sniffed the lad. 'I can't say no if Miss Allen wants to take out a horse even if the snow is proper deep.'

Prickles of unease ran down Felix's spine. Surely Phoebe hadn't been foolish enough to take her cream mare out into the winter weather.

'They can't have got far,' he said, trying to minimise his fear. 'Those little legs will be stuck in a snowdrift right outside the gate.'

Spiller's eyes were terrified.

'I'm so sorry, my lord, but Miss Allen hasn't taken her own mare.'

Felix's stomach turned to water.

'Lane, what horse did you saddle?'

'I'm sorry, my lord. I didn't know it were wrong. She's taken Kamil.'

His fear was so intense that Felix's heart and feeling were clear to him as never before: Phoebe was his life. It was difficult to maintain self-control and take care of his guest, but he managed to turn to the duke and speak calmly.

'Preston, you must forgive me. I

cannot think how Miss Allen can have been so foolhardy as to take Kamil, but I must rescue her.'

The duke was a kindly man, but not quick on the uptake. His benevolent brown eyes surveyed Felix.

'Do you have to rush off, old chap? I'm sure the young lady will turn back as soon as she realises how deep the snow is.'

Felix wished he could believe that. If only she would come riding through the arch back into the safety of the stable! But he knew that Phoebe wasn't likely to give up on any mission once she'd made up her mind to tackle it. She wouldn't consider turning back until she was dying and then it would be too late. He couldn't bear to think of Phoebe, his Phoebe, so bright and so sweet and so tiny, so incredibly tiny and vulnerable, alone on the moors.

'She's riding a horse that could turn vicious at any second. I must go after her.'

'I suppose your man could show me

the filly, but wait a minute; surely your man could go after the minx?'

'Not in this snow. It'll be six foot deep on top of the moors where the toymaker lives. The only horse with the strength to cope would be Shaitan, and I'll ask no one else to ride him.'

'I say, I thought the brute was too dangerous to ride.'

'I'd saddle the devil if he'd carry me to Phoebe,' Felix said grimly, heading for the paddock where the black stallion lived.

The duke toddled after Felix, but Spiller and young Tommy went running to the stables. By the time Felix had the gate open, Spiller had returned with a bridle and a bucket of oats and by the time Felix had caught Shaitan, Tommy had fetched his saddle and a whip.

Shaitan was bucking and plunging, showing the whites of his eyes as usual. Felix picked up his whip, showed it the horse and spoke sternly.

'I've never beaten you, my lad, but today you behave and do exactly as I tell you or I'll thrash you soundly. Do you understand?'

Shaitan's ears went forward and he regarded his master in utter astonishment.

'By Jove,' the duke exclaimed. 'That horse understood every word. Look how well he's behaving now. He's gentle as a lamb.'

'Be careful, my lord,' Spiller urged. 'Shaitan always takes careful handling and there's no saying how the snow will affect him.'

Felix knew all that, but he still mounted and urged the stallion out of the stableyard. He couldn't leave Phoebe alone in the icy wastes of the moors. He had to go and find her. He had no choice.

It was easy to follow the tracks in the glittering snow that Phoebe and Kamil had made. Felix's worry eased slightly when he saw that the hoof marks were evenly spaced, suggesting that the horse had been proceeding steadily and calmly up the white hill. A vivid blue sky soared over the white crest and the sun felt almost hot. He urged Shaitan on, and the horse galloped with a will, his great hooves sending up clouds of fine powdery snow.

The tracks led steadily onwards and upwards. Felix urged Shaitan to move even faster through the crisp air. The great stallion seemed happy to oblige and was intelligent enough to follow the tracks with very little guidance. He moved like silk under Felix, his long, strong legs breasting the glittering snowdrifts. Felix marvelled at the power beneath him. The horse seemed to be revelling in their mad dash.

His whole being was eaten up with fear for Phoebe. She'd only been riding for a few months. What if Kamil bucked her off and trampled on her? Even if the horse didn't turn vicious and savage her, there were so many other threats. What if horse and rider fell into a bog and were sucked under? The snow had blotted out all the familiar landmarks and she'd never even been to the cottage where the toymaker lived. What if she got off course and was lost in the wilderness and froze?

Felix knew that he couldn't live if she died. It was that simple. If only he hadn't been so distant with her. He should have realised how much she'd set her heart on the children having their toys on Christmas morning. If she came to grief over this mad escapade, he'd blame himself forever. He urged his horse on faster, so that he could see over the crest of the next fell, and there in the distance, tiny in the snow, was a moving black dot, coming towards them. He felt a surge of wonder and respect. She must have made it to the cottage and was now returning. Shaitan lifted his head and neighed.

'Phoebe!' Felix cried.

Phoebe was too weary to understand at first the significance of the horse's whinny that echoed across the billowing snow towards her, but Kamil halted for a second and neighed a reply. His reaction made her look up and across the dazzling whiteness. The dark shape she saw was still a long, long, way away, but she knew it was Felix. Who else would it be? She felt tears sting her eyes.

'Oh, thank you for coming,' she cried.

The wooden toys were heavy and her back felt as if it were breaking. Every muscle in her body ached. Kamil moved smoothly and behaved like a gentleman, but he was not her little pony and the motion of the enormous stallion was tiring. It had been many miles to the cottage and it seemed even further back. Her arms were shaking with the strain of balancing the sack in front of her, and she had been mortally afraid of dropping the toys and falling into a snowdrift. If she fell, it would be the end of her, for she hadn't the strength to wade through the drifts back to Elwood, but now all her fears lifted, for Felix was galloping towards her.

Felix was by her side in moments.

His green eyes were full of anxiety.

'You are exhausted. Give me that sack.'

She didn't want him to know how tired she was, but oh, she was so happy to let him take the burden from her.

'Why didn't Shackleton fix the toys to the saddle for you?'

Fighting the dizzy black clouds of fatigue, she lifted her head and met his gaze.

'He had no rope, no extra sacks, not even a satchel I could sling on my back. He had only this one sack.'

'What a hare-brained escapade!' Felix ejaculated.

His dark brows snapped together and his expression was momentarily ferocious. Phoebe eyed him cautiously.

'Are we . . . friends?'

He smiled, the dark lines of his face lifting into heart-breaking beauty. He reached out one hand and he touched her cheek, a tiny, fleeting, infinitely gentle gesture.

'What do you think?'

'I think you might be going to fly into a rage and chastise me for taking your horse.'

'No, I am too thankful to see that you are safe to lose my temper.'

'You see,' Phoebe couldn't resist telling him, 'whatever the provocation you never lose control.'

'What possessed you to take such a risk?'

'Unlike you, I did not think it was a risk. Kamil behaved well, just as I expected.'

'You were lucky.'

'It wasn't luck, it was Kamil's good nature. I told you I could trust him.' She examined his face. It was so full of lightness that she risked adding, 'As I am sure I can trust you.'

Felix guided Shaitan towards her, and then stopped in the snow when he was close enough to lean out of his saddle and take her hand. His clasp was warm and strong.

'It seems that your notions of horse breeding may be more accurate than mine. This morning, I received a letter from the bloodstock agent who sold me Shaitan. His former owner is notorious for mistreating his horses. He sold Shaitan because the stallion fought back. No wonder the poor beast has lost his faith in human beings. Although he has risen to the occasion today, I still wouldn't trust him far.'

'He doesn't have bad blood, and neither do his foals.'

'It would seem not. He and his bloodline are strong-willed, but how they turn out seems to be, as you speculated, more a matter of how they are treated.'

His manner was tender, and there was a world of love in his green eyes, so Phoebe felt free to cry passionately, 'Then won't you believe me when I say that you could never be like your father and that I trust you?'

'I do,' he said softly, and then he lifted his head and cried loudly, 'I believe you!'

She could see her feelings reflected in

his eyes: relief, passion and a joyous understanding of the possibilities that were opening out to them. He looked liberated, young, exhilarated.

'I am free of the past, thanks to you. Will you marry me, my dearest Phoebe?'

She looked up to meet Felix's green eyes, and she felt the warmth and the magic flowing around them.

'Yes, please!' she answered.

Phoebe smiled at him, and then she laughed out loud. Felix caught her mood. His green eyes filled with joy, but he caught her rein and guided Kamil towards Elwood.

'Come, you'll get cold. We must keep moving.'

As the horses crunched their way through the glittering snow towards Elwood, Felix looked at her and smiled.

'I have an engagement present for you that I think you will like.'

'This cannot be planned. Only yesterday you were so sure that you would never marry.'

'True, but I did want to give you a present. Don't you want to know what it is?'

Phoebe's heart swelled with happiness.

'I want only you. I don't need presents.'

His green eyes were full of love and delight because now he was free to make her happy.

'Not even Thomas Lawrence's portrait of your mother?'

Phoebe was too moved to speak, but as the horses crunched their way over the snow and back to Christmas at Elwood, warm magic flowed between the riders and their gazes met in a promise of a lifetime of trust, happiness and commitment.

Other titles in the
Linford Romance Library:

LADY EMMA'S REVENGE

Fenella J. Miller

Lady Emma Stanton is determined to discover who killed her husband, even if it means enlisting the assistance of a Bow Street Runner. Sergeant Samuel Ross is no gentleman; he has rough manners and little time for etiquette. So when Emma and Sam decide the best way to ferret out the criminal is to pose as husband and wife, they are quite the mismatched pair. Soon, each discovers they have growing feelings for the other — but an intimate relationship across such a social divide is out of the question . . .

STANDING THE TEST OF TIME

Sarah Purdue

When Grace Taylor wins a scholarship to study music at the exclusive Henry Tyndale School, she is determined to work hard to realise her dream of becoming a professional musician. There she meets the charming young Adam, and it feels like they were meant for each other — until a vicious bully with a wealthy father, to whom the school is beholden, succeeds in breaking them apart . . . Eight years later, fate throws Grace and Adam together again. Can they overcome the shadows of the past and make a life together?